The Village King

EDDIE MCGARRITY

Eddie McGarry

ISBN: 148107752X
ISBN-13: 978-1481077521

ALSO BY THE AUTHOR

Facebook.com/ElroodTheElf
@Elrood_the_Elf

Blog: eddiemcgarrity.blogspot

DEDICATION

Scott, Rob and Mike. But not necessarily in that order.
Or is it?

1

CLOUDS TUMBLED ACROSS a grey sky. Stephen pulled back his hood and allowed a light rain, the first for weeks, to patter on his hat. A few drops trickled down his neck. He kept his attention on the old farmhouse. Daylight was leaking away and a warm glow spread out from the window. Careless, he thought, of them to light a fire and not post a lookout.

On his way out he had looked the place over; abandoned, burnt out, and unused for months, maybe years. Now, three days later, on Stephen's way back in, the house was in use again. Unlikely to be the owner, he thought, who was probably long gone, more likely it was someone like him. Stephen lifted a scope to his eye. It was a small monocular, a Luger model he'd taken off a guy near Berwick, not far from where he crouched. It fitted neatly in his hand and gave him the spotter detail he needed without resorting to binoculars.

There was no movement from inside the building. Parts of the roof were still intact and the glow was from a sheltered part of the house. Stephen stowed the scope in a chest pocket and started to move back but stopped the moment he heard movement.

It was still pretty far away but he dared not move. He was in a hollow about 250 metres from the farmhouse, well back from the single-track road which led up to it. At the top of the road were four figures. When they came nearer, Stephen could see it was two men and two women. The women's hands were tied and they were being pushed down the road.

The group were about 50 metres from where Stephen crouched and he felt his throat tighten. The women had their heads bowed. They wore only light clothing, miserable in the rain, and their hair lay matted and dripping. Their feet were bare. The men were dressed, like Stephen, in good quality green outdoor gear. One of the men had a shotgun. Stephen fished out his scope again, and eyed the group, but couldn't make out if the other man was armed.

Stephen kept completely still as they passed by and finished their journey to the farmhouse. He was in a small fox-hole and knew they wouldn't spot him in the darkening air. The man with the shotgun called out to the farmhouse. Another man, dressed the same, came out to meet them. He laughed in surprised delight when he saw the women.

One of the women recoiled but she was shoved roughly in to the doorway. The second woman, shorter than the others, scrambled after the first and the whole group entered the farmhouse. Stephen saw movement in the room with the fire. Shadows flitted across the window frame. The men laughed and spoke to one another but Stephen couldn't make out what they were saying and there was no sound from the women.

He waited for a couple of minutes until he was sure they had settled then he pulled back from his fox-hole. It was filling with water and he was glad to be on the move. He thought of Ellen and Jack. *Bollocks*. Stephen looked at the farmhouse again.

He approached the farmhouse from the dark side. Rain continued to fall and he could still hear men's voices from inside. Nearer to the building, the ground became firmer, and Stephen padded up to the wall. From his previous visit he knew there was an open doorway up ahead and he silently approached.

He had stowed his overcoat and bag half a kilometre north, on his intended escape route, and had doubled back, hugging the eastern facing coastline. All he had was his Glock 26 pistol and large hunting knife. They would have to do. The pistol was fully loaded with 10 rounds. The short handle fitted neatly into his hand. He had readied a round before approaching and he now leaned his finger on the trigger. He stood by the open doorway and waited for his breathing to normalise. He was panicking and he needed to calm down. Storming houses was not his specialty.

He found a moment of calm and then entered. He kept the pistol pointed up like he'd seen in movies and used his left hand to feel his way round the darkness. He was in a kitchen. The appliances lay blackened and ruined amongst fire debris. Beyond the kitchen had been the hallway, and beyond that was the room with the fire and the men. He could hear their voices and their occasional laughter.

Rain poured into the hallway through the ruined roof. Stephen was grateful for it masking his footsteps as he treaded through the kitchen. Entering the hallway, his heart pounded. He kept his back to the wall just before the room with the men in it. Across from there was a cupboard. His senses shook when he realised two faces were looking at him.

It was the women though he saw that one of them was only a child. She lay frightened in the older one's arms. The woman, who Stephen now saw was of a similar age to him, still had her hands tied. She had hooked her arms around the girl for warmth but she held the girl closer now. They were both terrified.

Stephen pointed to himself then behind him, as if into the room, and shook his head. The older woman tensed. As if calculating something, she looked down at the girl then back at Stephen. She unclenched her fist and held out three fingers, which Stephen took to mean there were three men in the room. He nodded and then readied himself.

His eyes were beginning to adjust to the light. He was about to step into the room when one of the men suddenly lumbered out of the room. Stephen shrunk into the corner.

The man, filthy and bearded, belched and leered at the two women. "Alright, girls. Nearly time."

The man stopped when he felt Stephen press the pistol into the back of his neck and leaned his finger on the

3

trigger again. Stephen pushed harder and the man moved a little to the side. Stephen gambled a corner of his eye into the room and saw the two other men chewing on some food and ignoring the doorway. Before he could think of what to do, the first man roared and twisted round to grab Stephen's arm.

Stephen fired. The man howled and Stephen guessed he had only wounded him. He shouldered the man aside and stepped into the room. The man on the right had reached for the shotgun but Stephen was already preparing another shot, had his pistol steadied with his left hand, and had his feet planted. He dropped the man easily with a shot to the chest. The shotgun went off. As the man fell, the barrel lifted and it fired again. The third man, on the left, had jumped back into the corner, and held his hands up in fright.

"I'm not armed," he shouted. "Don't shoot."

Stephen turned back to the first man. He howled and rolled about on the floor, clutching his neck. Blood poured out of a wound. Stephen put a bullet in his head at close range then moved back into the room, sensing behind him the first man had gone still. He covered the man in the corner while he checked on the man with the shotgun. He lay gurgling on the floor, not moving.

Keeping his eye on the man in the corner, Stephen reached down and lifted the shotgun. The small fire crackled and burned. Stephen said, "Any more shells for this?" He held the shotgun up into the air.

The man in the corner was shaking with fright. Stephen repeated the question and stepped closer. The man recoiled but he whimpered something, gesturing to the opposite corner. Stephen was relieved to see it was a pile of canvas bags. He hadn't even checked that corner for people.

He angled his head towards the door. "You can come through now."

The women scrambled out of the cupboard and came

into the room, frightened and shivering. "Sit down by the fire," Stephen said to them. "Warm up for a bit."

Warily, the older woman moved nearer the fire. She dragged the girl, who kept her face hidden behind a curtain of hair. They crouched down next to the shotgun man who had stopped gurgling and lay silent. The woman found a small knife and began working at the girl's bonds.

"I wasn't going to hurt them," the man said. "It was their idea." He sat into the corner and his hands, though still raised, were shrinking back towards him.

Stephen wondered how he was going to do this. He needed whatever was in those bags but he couldn't risk taking his eye off this man. He put the shotgun down next to the bags. The woman had freed the girl and was now working on her own wrists. She had a hungry fire in her eyes, and Stephen didn't trust leaving the gun with her either.

He stepped up to the man in the corner and crouched down opposite him. Stephen could see he was young behind the beard, and genuinely scared. "What's your name, son?"

The man's voice was shaky. "Phil."

"How many of you are there, Phil?"

Phil frowned and he looked confused. Stephen asked patiently, "Are you expecting anyone else to join you?"

Phil shook his head quickly. "Just three of us."

"And who are they?" Stephen gestured to the dead men.

Phil shrugged. "Just some guys." Stephen thought there was something in the shrug which suggested Phil was glad to see the end of them and he hoped he wasn't just imagining it.

The woman and the girl tucked into a small pot of food which had been warming on the fire. The girl in particular wolfed into it. She must have been starving, thought Stephen.

"What's your name?" Stephen said to the woman. The

girl put down her food and moved behind the woman.

"None of your fucking business," said the woman. She spoke through a mouthful of food, unmistakably an Edinburgh accent. She swigged down some water from a canteen and passed it to the girl who drank deeply.

Stephen was suddenly angry. "Really? I just pulled your arse out a pantry."

"We never asked you to," the woman said and wiped her mouth. "Just gimme the shotgun and we'll be on our way." She reached over and tested the cloth of a coat which had been discarded on the floor near the shotgun man.

Stephen glanced at Phil. He seemed more frightened of the turn this conversation had taken than of Stephen. Phil swallowed and looked at the floor. He was hugging his knees.

Stephen sighed. "And where are you headed?" The woman shrugged.

When Stephen made eye contact with Phil, the younger man realised the question was meant for him too, so he said, "We just knock about here."

Stephen sighed. He began to relax, finding himself coming down from the fight. "There's a village further up the coast."

"So?" The woman glared at him. The girl rested her head on the woman's shoulder and gazed listlessly into the fire.

"So move yourself."

2

STEPHEN HAD PRESSED the muzzle against Phil's head while the boy raked through the bags. Amongst a load of crap was a tatty box with half a dozen shotgun shells in it. The woman and the girl cobbled together some more suitable clothing out of the crap. It was far too big for the girl, but the woman was pretty tall and broad. They used the dead men's boots.

While the girl clumped about, Stephen shook the box of shells at the woman and pointed at Phil, who was gathering a bag of his stuff. "Keep an eye on him." He handed her the box but kept a hold of the shotgun.

She eyed him up and down. She seemed to come to a decision inside herself and she nodded assent. He handed over the weapon. "Who's going to keep an eye on me?"

Stephen patted his holstered pistol. "I am."

"Why don't we stay here the night?" She cracked the shotgun open easily and popped the spent shells.

Stephen watched her practiced movements. "Someone might have heard the noise. We've been here too long as it is."

She nodded, eyeing him again. "Alana," she said then peered down the barrels. "I'm Alana. That's Karen."

"Your daughter?"

Alana jutted a chin at Phil as she thumbed two shells into the shotgun. "Your son?" When Stephen didn't say anything, Alana shrugged.

"I'm Stephen."

She shrugged again and lifted the shotgun's stock to meet the barrels and clicked the weapon into place.

They headed out to where Stephen had stowed his gear. The rain had stopped and a cold wind blew in from the sea, attacking the south east coast. It was dark but their eyes had adjusted. It was going to be tough going on the damp fields but they moved off anyway.

Stephen had recovered his backpack. It clanked heavily when he lifted it. Alana had eyed it, guessing at its contents. Phil led, told to walk "that way" keeping the sea to his right. Alana rested the shotgun on her arm, showing no sign of strain at the weight. Karen loped beside Alana while Stephen kept up the rear. The woman never looked over her shoulder. Stephen kept an eye on them all, inwardly kicking himself for getting involved. Their steps kicked through surface water as it tried to soak into the hardened ground.

3

PALENESS EMERGED ON their right. They could start
to make out the Bass Rock sitting in the sea further up the
coast. Stephen remembered mornings like this, getting
ready to go to school as the sun came up; Dad already at
work and Mum pouring a bowl of cornflakes. Back when
the world was right. He breathed in the sea air. It smelled
good, fresh.

The rest of his party was looking knackered. Phil was
exhausted and trudged grudgingly along the grass. The
going was a bit easier now but he made it look like hard
work. Karen didn't complain and she held onto Alana's
arm. The woman looked weary. He himself felt a bit better
now the sun was coming up, but the pack felt heavy. A can
was digging in his ribs.

They were reaching the crest of the rise when suddenly
Phil crouched down. Alana and Karen followed. Stephen
leaned over and he could see what the problem was. A
column of riders were heading out of the village and up the
road towards them.

"Morgan." He fell back a bit. Maybe they hadn't been
seen. He shouldered off the pack and hunted around
frantically. Everyone looked at him with panicked
expressions.

He found what he was looking for. To his left, a bush
covered over a small hollow. He beckoned them and they
scrambled over to him. He tipped his backpack out into the
hollow. Cans of food tumbled out. Alana gaped at the
contents then at Stephen. He said, "Those bastards will take
everything we have."

Alana understood immediately what he meant and she
cracked the shotgun and placed it gently in the hollow next
to the cans. Stephen tossed his pistol and knife in and he
and Alana covered it up as best they could with the bush.
Wide eyed, Phil moved into help. Karen kicked her boots

off under the leaves and Stephen motioned them all to follow him.

"Let's go," he said. A few cans clanked inside as he shouldered on his pack.

Alana tried to reach inside. "There's a few left."

"It's fine. If they search my bag, they might ignore the rest." Phil was looking back at the bush but Stephen knuckled his shoulder to straighten him up. They crested the hill again and made their way slowly down the hill for a couple of minutes before stopping by the road.

A few minutes after that, the first riders drew up just in front of them. Stephen muttered at them not to say anything. The Colonel, a man Stephen knew as Morgan, raised a hand to halt the column of twelve men and women. Morgan gestured to Stephen's party.

One of the soldiers dismounted and walked towards them. It was the female Sergeant, Stephen saw. Her rifle was in both hands crossed in front of her, the muzzle pointed at an angle to the ground. Behind her, two of the Privates clicked their weapons ready, lifted a foot over the horse's heads, and slid off to the ground.

Karen slunk behind Alana, who stood just behind Stephen's shoulder, and leaned into her arm. Phil stood off to Stephen's left, mouth open at the troops on horseback, their Multi Terrain Patten fatigues showed signs of wear, but were well maintained. The Sergeant was as tall as Stephen, and much broader than Alana, bulked out more by her sandy body armour. She looked out from inside the shade from her helmet. She never spoke, showing no sign of recognising Stephen. She looked at Karen's bare feet, then into Alana's eyes. She moved over to Phil and gestured with the rifle for him to move to the side. Two more Privates dismounted and ran up. One covered Phil, while the other pushed him around, moving him away from the others, and searched his bag.

The Sergeant kept her attention on Stephen, who tried

his best not to return a provocative gaze. Inside he was thinking, just a guy travelling through with his family. He wondered if she had recognised him and was just concealing it.

One of the Privates found something in Phil's bag and he stepped back triumphant. "Sergeant! Knife." He held up an old kitchen knife. Phil hung his head and sneaked a look at Stephen.

Stephen turned to Alana. A flicker in her eyes said she thought he was right to have kept an eye on Phil. He turned back to the Sergeant. "It's just a knife. He needs it."

The Sergeant reached out and roughly turned Stephen around. Alana moved Karen back a couple of paces. Noticing this, the Sergeant paused, and frowned briefly, before reaching into the back pack. Her gloved hand reached the cans, stopped and then she took her hand out and pushed Stephen in the back.

He turned around and glared at her. She stepped back and fingered the trigger of her rifle. Stephen breathed and made himself relax. The Sergeant kept walking backwards. She shook her head at the Private who held the knife. He sneered and tossed the knife and bag to the ground at Phil's feet. Phil carefully picked it up and made the short distance back to Stephen, who put a hand on Phil's shoulder but kept him at arm's length.

The Sergeant turned back to Morgan. "Nothing worth having, sir."

Morgan nodded, and kicked his horse forward. Stephen knew nothing about horses but he watched Morgan sit tall in the saddle, like some General from ages ago, too superior to look at them. The dismounted soldiers jumped back on their horses and the column moved out.

The Sergeant was last on and last in the line. She was the only one to look at Stephen and his party as the unit rode off down the road. Stephen nodded to her in gratitude at not taking the cans in his bag, knowing the soldiers had probably taken all they needed from the village; for now, anyway. He saw canteens on the side of their horses, bumping on their journey.

Stephen moved the other three off in the direction of the village and away from the soldiers. When he was sure they were far enough away, he turned and led everyone back to the hollow.

Nothing had been disturbed. Karen jumped into her boots. Phil absent-mindedly handed Alana the shotgun. Stephen fitted his holster back in place. "You should have left the knife here."

"I forgot," said Phil, seemingly genuinely ashamed. He looked off in the direction the soldiers had gone. "Who are they?"

"I dunno," said Stephen. He helped Alana with putting the cans into the pack. "Last of the Dreghorn barracks? They come into the village and steal everything those poor bastards have. Mostly they're there for the whisky."

"Whisky?" Alana zipped the pack up.

Stephen threw the pack onto his shoulders. "Yeah. The village is built round a distillery."

Alana helped him position the pack on his back. "I could do with a drink." She smiled and laid the shotgun over her left arm like a waiter and his towel.

"It'll cost you." He looked at her dead seriously. She knew what he meant. He was warning her, but not about himself.

Alana's face fell. They headed back to the road.

4

THE VILLAGE HAD been built like an old highland settlement. Intended as a tourist trap, Scotland's most southerly distillery had been constructed with the village around it. Just like some of the highland and island communities, the children had gone to school elsewhere, but there had still been a couple of shops, a church, and some houses.

The village sat nestled at the end of a broad hollow, Margaretvale, carved out by the river of the same name. The road in was single-track though its metalled surface had sprouted weeds. Morgan's horses were the only traffic now. A cattle-grid marked the start of the village; its thin strips of steel laid over a shallow hole in the ground. On the right was the parish church; an old building left over from a much older settlement. The manse, the minister's traditional house, sat back from it in front of the newer village hall.

Further on from that was the Excise cottage, a throwback to an era when Her Majesty posted men to watch over the whisky. Behind the Manager's house next door was a scattering of houses where most of the people lived. Across the street were the Police Station, shop, tea room, barbers, and a row of faux wash-houses; as if the women of the parish still worked their laundry there.

The wash-houses faced the church and brought you back to the cattle grid. Turn right and you go down a steep hill to the whisky distillery which sits right above the shore. The road leads past long tall warehouses on either side. The sea facing walls had been painted with the name of the distillery, Glen Craobhmore; pronounced Krav-more. It means valley of the big tree and refers to the forestry commission planted trees which covered the hills beyond the broad hollow. Like most of the village, the name is a construct of the imagination.

Past the warehouses is the Distillery itself, separated

from the warehouses by the road to the broad pier. Jutting out into the sea, the pier was to evoke the past when grain boats used to visit distilleries but it functioned really as a tourist harbour for visiting yachts.

Boats no longer come to the village, but before things went bust, you could moor up, visit the distillery and take a stroll up the path from the plant to the shop and tea room.

5

STEPHEN AND HIS group approached the village. He had waved on their approach, knowing Gareth would have been watching through his binoculars and recognises him.

Sure enough, Gareth was on duty atop the gate, ten metres up from the cattle grid. He looked down at them from the tangle of wire and bricks. "Not more mouths, Stephen. You can feed them if you like."

"Just open the gate." Stephen was weary from the travelling and the stress. The others stood nervously around him. He looked around. The gate only stopped things coming down the road. The countryside was wide open, and they could have just walked round it if they liked, but Stephen indulged Gareth on this issue. He saw Alana looking at the hoof prints of Morgan's unit which churned up the ground around the gate.

Gareth turned away and jumped down, disappearing from view. They heard a scraping sound and a small opening appeared as some of the structure was swung back. Stephen ducked down and went under. Alana pulled Karen by the hand and Phil followed.

Straightening, Stephen greeted Gareth's wife, Bet, with a nod. Broad and stern-faced, she held a baseball bat and eyed the shotgun crooked over Alana's arm. She softened when she saw Karen, all skinny with clothes draped over her.

Gareth and his son, Derek, pushed the gate back into place, plugging the gap. Phil stood in wonder at the gate, like he'd seen nothing like it. Gareth said, his tone exasperated, "Suzanne will want to know you've brought new folk in."

Stephen sighed. "Look Gareth. I know you're pissed off 'cause Morgan's just been and rode round your poxy gate, but don't tell me what to do." He pulled Alana's shoulder and they walked through a small open gate next to the cattle gird. Metal bars strapped over a shallow hole in the ground kept the few grazing cows inside the village now instead of out.

Stephen's billet was in the wash-houses just to the left. They walked round the building. A young man, with close-cropped hair, sat on a folding lawn-chair, facing out to sea. He grinned when he saw Stephen then baulked when he saw the others. He jumped to his feet and bounded over. He wore green camouflage trousers, and a khaki shirt, both of which had originally been from a fashion store. Karen stared at dog tags round his neck. He shook Stephen's hand. "Good to see you back. You alright?" He looked at the people with Stephen. His accent was like Alana's, Stephen suddenly realised, unlike his own Dumfries and Galloway tones.

"It's a long story, Gary," said Stephen, referring to the people he had brought in. He unhooked his backpack. Gary admired its heaviness, knowing what was in it. Stephen introduced everyone. Phil was wary of Gary, but he shook his hand. Karen hid behind Alana's legs.

When Gary shook Alana's hand, he said, "Nice shotgun."

"Yeah, sorry Gaz," said Stephen."It's hers." He jerked a thumb at Alana. "Any trouble?"

Gary shrugged and smiled openly with white teeth. "Rory came sniffing about, but I handled him."

"Good." Stephen thought for a moment. He nodded for Gary to move off with him, leaving the others behind. They leaned on the wall which separated the wash-houses from a drop to the warehouses below. "Can you billet, Phil?"

Gary breathed in, and rubbed his arm. He looked over at the group who waited quietly. "Sure. You looking for some quiet time with the woman?"

Stephen sniggered. "I think she would take that shotgun and blow my head off." They fell silent for a moment, and looked out at the blank horizon, until Stephen asked,

"Morgan?"

Another shrug. "That lady Sergeant poked around. They spent a day in the warehouse, mostly. And they killed another one of the cows."

Stephen sighed and shook his head. "These poor bastards'll have nothing if this keeps up."

Gary leaned in closer, glancing at Stephen's group. "Three more mouths, Stephen."

Stephen nodded, conceding the point. "Just keep an eye on Phil. He's got a knife. I'll tell you the whole story later."

"You need a kip?"

"I think we all do." Stephen made it sound like a question.

"Me too," yawned Gary, stretching. "I've been up for a least a couple of hours."

6

STEPHEN HEATED UP a large tin. It was marked beef stew and the smell filled the small room. Karen sat in front of the fire, staring at the pot as the contents started to bubble. Alana sat next to her. She had been put off by the rumple of covers on a mattress in the corner and sat with her back to the mess. Through her eyes, Stephen saw it for what it was; a hovel.

"It's not much of a place," he said, and stirred the stew with a metal spoon. It scraped along the bottom of the pot. He and Gary had arrived separately but each had taken over one of the wash-houses. Handily, the designers had put in old ranges; fires with metal plates for cooking food. The pot rested on one of the plates, while a battered old kettle sat on the other, heating some water.

"It's warm," she said.

He could tell she was trying to be pleasant and he noticed her glance again at his bed. "I've not lifted you out of there, just to bring you somewhere worse." He picked up one of the small plates, spooned in some of the stew and handed it to Karen. "Or the same."

Alana eyed him. "So why did you?" She watched Karen eat, and kissed her on the head. Stephen handed her a plate of stew. She bowed her head in gratitude, closed her eyes, moved her mouth as if saying something, then opened her eyes and ate.

Stephen used the big spoon and ate straight from the pot. He was careful with it, chewed each piece, and licked the spoon clean. He thought of Ellen and Jack, but never answered her. She noticed that, so asked him something else. "What is this place?"

"Just a village," said Stephen. "They live pretty quiet, but they're menaced by the soldiers and the folk in the forest make it a pain in the arse to get wood."

Alana put her arm round Karen. The girl just stared into

the fire. She was very protective of her younger charge, he thought, and he had just cursed the room out. "Sorry."

"I swore first," said Alana. "It's just having something hot to eat makes it seem, dunno, normal." She'd searched for the last word. Stephen knew what she meant. Their life was tough, had been since the virus, and it had made them tough. Domesticity showed how coarse they had become.

Through her eyes again, he saw himself. He was filthy. His hair was knotted and his beard was unkempt. Tomorrow, he would sort himself out. There was a great big porcelain sink in here after all. The water system still worked.

The kettle boiled and Stephen used a tea bag for the three of them. He had some chipped mugs. Karen was fascinated by the process but she pulled a face when she tasted some of it.

"It's better with some milk and sugar," Stephen laughed. He handed Alana her mug and she breathed in the steam. She sipped gratefully.

"Where did you find tea bags?"

"Trade secret." He sipped at his. It was hot. He'd found them in an old B&B outside Jedburgh and had been hanging onto them ever since, doling them out to himself and Gary.

Karen crawled over to the mattress and slid in between the covers. Alana went to stop her, but Stephen said, "It's okay. You can use that too if it's not too disgusting. I'll kip here."

Alana sipped her tea and sighed in approval. When she'd finished, she slid in beside Karen, but not before she'd artfully positioned the loaded shotgun within reaching distance. She quickly dropped off to sleep.

7

STEPHEN WOKE UP as the door closed. Alana had closed it gently but it lifted him out of sleep all the same. He was sore from having slept on the hard floor. It was just getting light. The bed was empty. Alana and Karen, and the shotgun, had gone but they had left their coats.

He managed to stand up and sucked in cold air and blew it out again. He leaned into the fire. It was still warm. He'd thrown a log on in the middle of the night to keep it going. He reached for a few sticks he kept in a wood basket and hoped they would catch. He grabbed the kettle and filled it in the sink, pulling the curtains back. Outside, he could see Alana, looking around with the shotgun crooked over her arm. Stephen scratched his head and felt grateful she hadn't shot him during the night. Karen looked like she was bursting and bounced up and down on the path.

Stephen rapped his knuckles on the window and caught Alana's attention. When she turned, he pointed towards her left and crooked his finger round like he meant for her to go round the corner. She looked at where he was gesturing. When she saw what he was pointing to, she turned back and gave him the thumbs up and a surprised look. He had sent her to the public toilets, originally built for the tourists.

Chuckling, he filled the kettle. It made him need to visit the toilets too, conveniently sited at the end of the wash-house. Placing the kettle back on the hob, Stephen saw the sticks were starting to catch. He poked around with another stick then built it up a bit, placing wood carefully to keep air flowing through. It started to spark and catch.

The door opened again. Alana breezed in, followed by Karen who looked more at peace, and quite subdued. "Toilets? You've got everything here."

Karen skulked over to the mattress and plonked herself down on it. Alana placed the shotgun down on the floor, well away from Stephen.

Stephen gestured to the shotgun. "You won't need that walking about the village."

Alana looked at the gun, then up at him blankly. He added, "Not unless you step on their grass, though."

She burst out laughing. Karen looked at Alana with a puzzled expression. Stephen excused himself and stepped outside. Gary's billet was still quiet. It was still early, but he thought he better check if everything was okay. He banged on the door and nipped to the toilet.

When he came back, he banged on the door again. Bleary eyed, and squinting in the daylight, Gary cracked the door. "I'm up, I'm up." Stephen looked inside and saw Phil stir under a mess of blankets.

"Everything okay?"

"Yeah, yeah," said Gary, stepping out onto the path. He had no boots on but had slept in his clothes and he shouldered on a green jacket. He tiptoed off to the toilet.

"I've got the kettle on," Stephen called after him. "Phil? Breakfast, son."

There was a groan of agreement so Stephen left him to it and went back next door. Inside, Alana was kneeling down in front of the fire. He saw it had started to go out but she was nurturing it back into existence.

8

AFTER BREAKFAST OF a couple of cans of beans shared between the five of them, Stephen got them ready to go for a walk round the village. "I'll show you about."

Alana went to lift the shotgun but Gary motioned to stop her. "They won't like you walking round with that."

She gave a look that asked him why she should give a shit. Gary laughed out loud. "I'm just saying." Then he had a think and looked at Stephen, who shrugged agreement. Gary said, "Look, I like the shotgun. Maybe we could trade."

"Trade?" Alana was sceptical. Karen sat on the mattress and folded her hands patiently. Phil was agog.

Gary reached under his jacket to the waistband of his trousers and unclipped a holster. He held it out to her. "Trade."

She paused, reading the situation. With the shotgun still on the floor behind her, she took the holster from Gary and pulled out a small pistol. It was a Glock 26 and, like Stephen's, it had been liberated from two dead policemen near Morpeth.

Stephen had seen Alana expertly reload a shotgun, but he still asked, "You know how to use that?"

She ignored him and handed Karen the holster. She removed the clip, saw it was full, racked the slide a couple of times to check it was empty then dry fired it towards the fireplace. It clicked sweetly. Alana held the gun out at arm's length and checked the sights. Gary and Stephen looked at each other, probably thinking the same thing.

"Where'd you learn to do that?" Stephen asked.

She looked at him, the hint of a smile at the sides of her mouth. It seemed to Stephen that she liked to keep him guessing. Five years of surviving, he thought, made you keep a few secrets. She palmed the magazine back in and took the holster off Karen, placing the pistol carefully in.

She came to a decision. "Trade this gun as is for the shotgun?"

"Oh, yes," said Gary but Stephen saw he'd fallen for her trap though he said nothing, amused.

"Well, help yourself" said Alana, holding onto the pistol but still keeping herself between Gary and the shotgun. "You'll be wanting some shells too? Trade?"

"What?" Gary was mad and he shuffled on his feet, looking to Stephen.

Alana said, "Two more pistol bullets for each shell I've got."

Stephen saw Alana had her hand on the grip ready to pull the pistol. "You're taking advantage of our good nature."

Phil had shuffled into the back corner. Karen just sat with her hands folded.

"What makes you think we've even got that many bullets?" Gary had backed off physically but he was just as angry.

"Oh, I think you boys have got stuff." Alana looked at the ajar door. She stepped between the men and pushed it shut. She looked out the window as if looking for someone. "I think you've got stuff but you need more to get you through the winter."

Stephen and Gary looked at each other. Gary's eyes betrayed she was right. Alana said, "Thought so. Those tins you brought in. I reckon there's more of them but you have to leave one person here while you go out alone. Want to hear an idea?"

Stephen didn't want to let her know she was right but when she had tested the pistol he and Gary had both realised there may be a way round their predicament of having to be here to guard their stash, while the other went out alone. "I'm all ears."

Alana shifted her weight from one foot to another. "You leave me and Karen here to guard your stuff. The three of you go and get as much as you can carry. We'll need it for the winter. Deal?"

Stephen looked at Gary. The younger man had cooled and he looked resigned, grudgingly agreeing it made sense. Stephen said, "We'll think about it."

"Okay, okay," said Alana. "But the bullets."

Gary agreed with a curt nod and a sigh. "Give me the shells now and I'll go get your bullets."

Alana made a show of considering it but she lifted her head at Karen who reached into her coat and brought out the tatty box of shells and shook them at Gary. He snatched them off her and lifted the shotgun. As he left the room, nudging Alana with his shoulder, Phil went to get up and follow. Stephen raised a hand to stop him. He didn't want Phil seeing what Gary was doing and where he stashed the shotgun.

"So," said Alana, breathing deeply in relief. "We going for that walk or what?"

9

THEY WALKED THROUGH the high street, leaving the wash-houses, the village hall and parish church behind. Phil and Gary walked up ahead while Karen held onto Alana and Stephen showed them the sights.

The old tea-room sat abandoned, its windows broken and the contents trashed inside; Morgan. Jeff's Barber's shop was still in the business of trading haircuts for produce and cutting soldiers' hair. Standing in the doorway, Jeff nodded to Stephen and smiled at the new woman and child, no doubt calculating Stephen's business. Iqbal's shop was empty but the door lay open as usual, facing the Police Station. Across the street, the Excise House was quiet but they could see a couple of figures, Dan and Jackie, tending their plot. The door of the Manager's House was thrown open and Suzanne ran out.

"Good morning, Stephen," she said pleasantly. "And who do we have here?" She leaned on her knees and smiled at Karen. The girl hid behind Alana.

Stephen introduced them, pointing out Phil who had wandered off with Gary behind Suzanne's place to the other houses. Suzanne had been the Manager at the distillery and had assumed the leadership of the village. She shook hands with Alana, whose tough demeanour contrasted with Suzanne, her larger frame having shrunk inside her casual wear. Alana said nothing.

After the introductions, Suzanne's eyes narrowed at Stephen. "Three more mouths? You can feed them if you like."

"Funnily enough that's what Gareth said," smiled Stephen, thinking how much influence she had here. "You worry about your business and I'll worry about mine."

Suzanne allowed her head to lean back and a corner of her mouth pulled back into a sort of smile. Not for the first time, Stephen saw the toughness there, the unwillingness to back down. It was what had helped this place survive five years, he thought.

"Do you think it will rain, Stephen?" she asked him directly.

Stephen said, "Couldn't say but it rained a bit further south yesterday,

"Well, it was lovely to meet you," said Suzanne, switching into sweet old lady mode to end the conversation. She waved at them as they moved on. "You come and see me with a few of your tins, why don't you?"

After a quick look at the village houses behind Suzanne's place, they picked up Gary and Phil, and went back to the high street and headed for the path between the Police Station and Iqbal's shop. Paul, the only officer of the law left, stepped out the Station door and leaned on the frame. He was chewing something and he watched them without saying anything. Stephen ignored him as they walked past him. Karen was fascinated with his worn and frayed uniform.

Gary and Phil bounded down the steps which were placed in short bursts in between the longer, twisting, ramp. Alana and Karen followed Stephen down the gentler path. Alana asked, "What is the script with this place? It's so untouched."

"Believe me, it's been touched," said Stephen. He gestured out to the horizon. The sea was flat calm and it met the grey sky at an empty thin line. "It looks nice. But the virus got most of the place, teams of tough guys got some more. People left, I think, but they've picked up other people."

"People like you?"

"Oh, there's no-one like me," he said. She smiled at him, a reward for trying to be charming. "But Morgan and his men showed up a year ago and are slowly picking it clean. See here?" He pointed to where the path ended at an open area of grass land which had three cows grazing on it. "This whole village was covered with cows seemingly. Morgan's men have butchered most of them."

They arrived at the grassy area, which sat just above a pebble shoreline. The cows looked at them. Fascinated, Karen moved towards them. Alana pulled her back. The girl didn't resist. Stephen looked over at Gary and Phil loping through the distillery, then turned back to Karen. "She never says much."

"She does to me." Alana kept her side to Stephen, not meeting his eyes. He tried not to think of what they must have gone through just to get here. He let it drop. He tapped her on the arm and they followed him to the distillery.

The plant itself was a few small buildings inside a courtyard. Tall wooden gates, closed and locked, faced them. Paintwork flaked at the lettering above: Glen Craobhmore. The three of them just looked at it like they were tourists on a summer day. Behind them, the pier plupped on the water as the tide shushed against the shore. To their right was the road between the warehouses. They heard slow footsteps.

Stephen turned around. Alana was already reaching for her pistol which was concealed in her coat and she had stepped in front of Karen. Stephen placed his hand on her arm, which made her stop drawing the weapon further, but she held her hand where it was. Three men were walking towards them; one straight on while the two others spread out in a flank.

Stephen spoke first. "What do you want, Rory?"

The middle man smiled but he stopped walking. "To say hello." He looked Alana up and down. "You've found two women, eh?"

"Fuck off, Rory." It was Gary. He had stepped around from the sea-facing wall of the East Warehouse. Phil followed, and Stephen noticed a sudden difference in him. Gone was the frightened boy they'd had for two days. In his place was a tough-guy used to squaring up behind his mates.

Rory hadn't expected Gary to be there, let alone have someone with him, but he held his position. Deek and Tim, the other two, shuffled nervously. Stephen kept his face neutral but he spoke as if to a child, "You heard the man, Rory."

This riled Rory, and he sneered, almost to himself; his top lip curling slightly. He pulled back. "Come on." Deek and Tim trotted after him and the three headed off towards the path.

Alana relaxed her hand. "You better watch him."

Stephen snorted. "He's nothing."

"I'm not sure about that. He's had lifetime of indignities. Bullied at school. Pushed around at work. You watch him."

10

THEY MOVED DOWN to the pier. An older stone jetty led from the shore into the sea beside them. Seaweed reached out from low tide and covered half of it. The pier they were on was crumbling concrete but it was safe enough. It took them out to the jetty which could be found by going through an open gate and down a wooden ramp to tidal pontoons. Empty basket creels lay stacked and drying at the end. There were no boats.

Karen stepped up to the water and looked in. Alana let go of her hand and allowed her to lie on the wooden surface and run her hand through the cold water. Stephen sat down on the edge and tapped the soles of his boats in the sea. Alana tucked hair behind her ears and joined him.

Gary and Phil had disappeared again and walked along in front of the East Warehouse. It was about 100 meters long and had been painted "Glen Craobhmore" in large letters to be seen from the sea.

"I can't remember the last time I saw a boat," said Alana.

Stephen kept looking out to sea. He liked it there. It was quiet and today was perfect, despite the cool early autumn air. "What do you miss the most?" he asked her.

She stroked Karen's back, almost ready to grab her coat if the girl began to slip into the water. She shook her head and gave a down-turned smile. "Nothing. We're free now, you know? Everything that happened has finished. We can do anything now."

She looked straight at him. He felt like she was telling him that she didn't want to share anything of her true self and that she didn't want to know his story either. But it was like she was telling him something else, too. He started to think about her back on the mattress then he thought of Ellen. She was like Ellen.

He jumped up and startled Karen. Alana breathed in and

followed, dragging the girl. "We can come back later."

As they headed up the jetty a small man walked towards them with a pole over his shoulder. He smiled when he saw Stephen. "I heard you were back."

"Hey, Frank," said Stephen and they shook hands. He introduced the girls.

"I've heard all about you," said Frank. He leaned down towards Karen. "I'll teach to fish if you like."

Karen turned her nose up at him, despite his friendliness. Frank swallowed. Stephen said, "Catch one for me, Frank."

"I'll see what I can do, lad. I'll see what I can do." Frank gave them a cheery single wave then went off to the end of the pontoons. He called back, "Do you think it will rain?"

"You'll be fine," Stephen shouted back.

He led them on the road through the warehouses. All were locked, like the distillery, but a few of the doors had bullet holes in them. "Rory from back there controls the keys to this place. But he pisses himself when Morgan's unit arrive and he lets them take as much as they like."

"Soldiers," Alana spat. "They must have made a dent in the inventory."

They met up with Gary and Phil who'd been like two small boys playing on the beach. All five climbed the road which swept them back to the cattle-grid and the wash-houses.

11

THEIR EVENING MEAL was a large tin of hot dogs followed by a can of sliced-peaches. Their mouths watered at the smell when Stephen opened the afters. He held it in the middle of them and they all crowded round, looking at the golden fruit swimming in syrup. He handed it to Gary on his left. Gary smelled the contents then passed it to Phil to do the same. Stephen smiled encouragement at him so Phil did as Gary had done, smelled the contents and passed it to Alana.

Once they'd all done that, Karen handed it back to Stephen. He met Alana's gaze. "Ladies first?"

Alana smiled broadly. "Youngest to oldest."

Gary nodded agreement. Stephen held out the can. Karen reached in with her spoon and fished out a slice. She sniffed it then nibbled a piece. She smiled coyly at Alana then disappeared from the group and nibbled at the morsel. Phil and Gary took a slice before Stephen lifted one out. He passed the can to Alana. "Youngest to oldest."

Phil and Gary sniggered into their spoon. Alana lifted a slice out. "Cheeky."

They finished the tin and sat back against the walls, happy and full. Karen curled up under the blanket and dozed off. In silence, they sat and watched the fire crackle. Stephen and Gary had spoken privately earlier, so he spoke up. "I've been thinking about your idea."

Alana toyed with her spoon. The handle had been warped and bent. She ran her fingers across it. "Really?"

Gary repositioned his feet and stared at the floor. Stephen went on. "There's a place where there are more un-disturbed tins than even three of us can carry."

"Where?" Alana asked quickly.

"So you can creep out at night?" said Gary.

"And you catch me in there? Don't be stupid." Her voice was filled with contempt.

"You wouldn't find it even if we told you," Stephen went on, lowering his voice. Alana watched him carefully. "Gary and me will go. The three of you will stay here."

"No way," Alana said. She glanced at Phil, who sat quietly next to Gary.

"You'll keep an eye on this place, and on each other. No-one gets in here. You make sure of that."

Gary added, "And if you mess with our stuff, we'll be back. You couldn't run off."

"Do you think?" Alana leaned forward provocatively. "Five years I've made it before I bumped into you."

Stephen leaned over and spoke as icily as he could. "But this is the first winter you've got the chance to be safe."

Alana sighed. "Okay. What about this? Gary and Phil stay. We go to the site."

Stephen didn't need to look to Gary. "No deal. This is the deal. Nothing else. We go. The location stays secret-"

"Secret." She shook her head

"-until we can trust you. There will be other runs."

She nodded, still thinking. She turned to Phil and pointed. "But you look at either of us the wrong way, sunshine, and I'll rip your head off." She sighed out her anger and turned to Stephen. "When?"

"We stock up on wood tomorrow, then we go." Stephen looked around for agreement. No-one argued.

12

IN THE MORNING, Stephen took Phil and Gary down
to the barber's. He had given them a can each but Jeff had
accepted Stephen's first offer of one tin of stew for the
haircuts and shaves. Gary's hair was already pretty close
cropped despite Jeff only being able to use scissors but both
Stephen and Phil had long hair and unruly beards. They sat
at the window while Gary had his hair cut first.

When Jeff had finished, Gary rubbed his nearly bald
head. Stephen laughed. "It's right into the wood, son."

Jeff used an open razor to shave Gary. When he was
done, Phil quietly asked for the same look. It took ages but
when Jeff had finished, Phil looked like a boy again. Gary
slapped him on the head. Phil recoiled but he smiled slyly.

After Stephen's hair cut and beard trim, he thanked Jeff
and left him to sweep up the mounds of hair on the floor.
Sheepishly, Phil reached into his coat and pulled out the
small tin of beans Stephen had given him. He nodded once
to Jeff and put it on the counter next to the front door. Jeff
looked open mouthed at it.

"What did you do that for?" Gary shoved Phil on the
shoulder. They walked back up the street towards the wash-
houses.

"He did a good job," Phil shrugged.

Stephen stopped Phil. He rubbed his trimmed beard,
little more than stubble, and said, "Every tin we have helps
us through the winter."

Phil nodded his head lower. Stephen clasped him behind
the head. They resumed their walk.

As they approached the wash-houses, they could see
some activity. The kids from the village were kicking a ball
about in front of the hall. Seven of them, they had a range
of ages, all under twelve. Stephen could tell they were
interested in Karen but the girl leaned against the wall,

watching them quietly.

Further on, Alana was draping wet blankets on the wall, careful they didn't drop down the cliff beyond. She did a double take when she saw the three of them. "That's better. Was that so difficult?"

Stephen and Gary laughed. Phil shrunk a bit. Stephen said, "Are these my blankets?"

"They were disgusting. You've got running water, you know" she said. Gary laughed. Straight faced, she said to him, "I doubt yours are much better." Gary stopped laughing and made a wry smile at Stephen. But she softened suddenly, "If you bring me your clothes I'll do them too. You got a change?"

Stephen looked at the three of them through her eyes. They were just as bad as the blankets. "We should match our new haircuts."

He went to walk by her, but she placed a hand on his chest. "Not in there. I'm going to sweep it out. You can get washed in Gary's."

Stephen smiled at her on one side of his mouth. "Yes, ma'am."

The children's ball rolled down and rested at Karen's bare feet. She just looked at it.

13

STEPHEN LED THEM out of the village. He ignored Gareth and Bet to take a line straight from the cattle grid. Leaving Gareth's gate to their left, they stepped onto the grass and headed towards the forest. Gary was left sitting on his folding chair outside the wash-houses. Stephen had intended on taking just Phil but Alana had insisted. She "wanted to see the forest." Karen, of course, loped after them in her oversize boots.

Phil was dressed in identical fatigues to Gary but he needed the hood up on his coat to keep off the morning cold. The two of them looked like new recruits to the cadets. Stephen realised he felt good to be dressed in his own clean clothes; having had them washed and dried by Alana. They followed a slight depression in the grass which had once been a track, now overgrown.

An hour later, they arrived at the edge of the forest, next to the Margaretvale River. They all shouldered off their bags and packs. Evidence of the forest having been worked was all around them. Trees had been felled, leaving a ragged edge to a planned forest. Stephen said to Karen, "Can you look for twigs and small branches that are on the ground?"

Without directly agreeing, Karen started hunting around. She found a few small branches and began to gather them up. Stephen said to Alana, "Watch the tree line." She set her jaw, nodded, and began to help Karen.

Stephen fetched a small axe he had in his backpack and he gave it to Phil to start chopping at a short tree. The boy made short work of it and it soon tumbled over. He stepped back, and wiped sweat from his brow and undid his coat. Stephen took over and began to hack at the branches with the axe.

"Stephen." Alana had kept her voice low and calm but he knew straight away that he was to look up.

A group of five people emerged from the trees. Their

clothes were ragged and their faces were blackened by soot and grime. They moved slowly, curious at their visitors, but they didn't venture far, keeping the trees to their backs. Stephen could see the group was made up of two men and three women. One of the men was older and stood slightly in front of the others. Stephen stood up and he felt Phil lining up behind him. Karen ducked behind Alana's legs while Alana reached towards her pistol, her hand hovering ready to draw.

The group of people stopped, and the older man shouted, "Who are you people?"

"We're from the village," said Stephen. He'd had this conversation before with people in the forest. "We're here for wood."

The older man stepped away from the group. The others did not move. "These are our trees. The wood, the food, the animals in the trees are ours."

Stephen looked over to Alana, saying quietly, "This is normal. Relax." She looked back at the group of people, an evil look in her eyes. Stephen called out, "We don't need much. We'll be gone soon."

The older man closed the gap but he kept about ten paces between them. "You people from the village, with your houses and your new clothes, are not welcome here."

Stephen kept his eye on the man but he imagined how they looked to this man from the forest. In their clean garments and barbered hair they must have looked soft to these people. He said, simply, "Alana."

At his prompt, Alana drew the Glock. She pulled back the slide to ready a shot and held out the pistol with her left hand cupped under her right.

A small smile crept onto the older man's face. "I am Joseph," he said. "Remember my name."

Joseph backed off and he and his people melted into the forest. They never came back the rest of the time Stephen's group gathered wood, but he imagined their eyes watching them from the gloom.

14

ON THE MORNING they were due to leave on the can run, Stephen was woken by a bell. A hand-rung bell rang from outside, insistent and deliberate, raising the alarm. Stephen jumped up. Across the room, Alana stirred before sitting up. "What is it?" she asked.

Stephen pulled his trousers on and stepped outside, still buckling his belt. He looked up at the hills above the village and saw what the bell was for. It was Morgan's Unit. The small column of soldiers, all still on horseback, had crested the hill and were making their way down the road. Gareth, doing his job on the gate, had spotted them, and was ringing the bell to let everyone know.

Alana and Karen appeared at his side. She swore when she saw the soldiers and ushered Karen back inside, but the girl brushed by to use the toilet. Gary and Phil joined them outside. Gary rubbed his head and yawned. Phil looked terrified.

Stephen said, "You all battened down there?"

"Yup, all locked down." They had stacked all the wood up, inside Gary's, in front of their supplies and weapons; Gary's shotgun included. After moving in, Gary and Stephen had removed part of a wall, lifted some floorboards, and had stashed their stuff there. Morgan's men would likely mooch about but not actually disturb their home, let alone piles of wood. At least, they normally did that, thought Stephen.

"Will you still go today?" Alana asked.

"Nah. We'll stick around," said Stephen. "We'll see what they do."

Karen skipped up and Stephen gestured for them to go into their respective billets.

Morgan's Unit rode round the gate and pulled up around the church. With the manse, the former Minister's home, just behind it, the churchyard and garden provided a decent sized pasture for the horses. Stephen and Alana watched discreetly from a small window as Morgan dismounted.

Tall and broad, and though he was dressed the same as his unit in the Multi-Terrain-Pattern uniform, he alone wore a soft teal-coloured beret, where the others wore helmets. He wore two silver pistols at his belt, like a mad general of old, thought Stephen. The rest of the unit wore helmets, which they began to unclip and hook under an arm, relaxed in their environment. Morgan strode about, surveying the manse. One of his men took his horse away to join the others.

Quietly, though they would not be heard, Alana said to Stephen, "I'd like to know what their story is."

Stephen made a non-committal shrug, "Would it make a difference?"

She looked him in the eye. "I came across a unit like this last year. They'd gone rogue because they had no command structure. This guy Morgan is clearly in charge."

"So?"

"So, why are they leeching off the people when they're supposed to be helping them?"

"Fair point." Stephen looked back outside. Morgan was pointing at the house, talking to two men. "The one on the left is Captain Weaver and the other one is Lieutenant Baxter."

"And we already met the Sergeant." Alana brushed up next to Stephen as she tried to see out the small window. "Do they always do this?"

"No. My guess is Colonel Morgan is sizing up a winter home."

Alana drew away and put her back to the wall. "Soldiers here for the winter? Bad news."

"And a re-think on the can runs."

Alana chewed her lip. "Could we stay where the cans

are?"

Stephen shook his head. "I wouldn't have when these goons were out in the countryside. Maybe now."

She moved back to the window and looked out. Stephen hung back and looked at her. Long hair, dark mostly but with different colours flavouring the effect, surrounded the pale skin of her face. Her eyes were brown and she watched intently. He asked her, "Why are you interested in their story?"

She shrugged. "Just interested." Alana didn't look at him but kept her attention on the soldiers outside.

She was lying, he knew. There was something else, he thought, maybe she had been in the military. Certainly, she knew how to fire a gun. He said, by way of drawing out her thoughts, "I'll tell you what I've been wondering."

"What?" She still didn't look at him.

He paused. "What would happen if their command structure was disrupted?"

"What do you mean?"

"What if Morgan was taken out? What would the outcome be?"

This time she looked at him.

15

MORGAN CALLED A meeting and everyone gathered in the hall. Children were supposed to wait outside but Karen had clung to Alana, who stayed next to Stephen in a spot against the wall but still near the door. Gary and Phil stayed at the wash-houses. Finally, the adults from the village gathered, all fifty three of them.

Suzanne sat on a chair at the end. The floor of the hall had once been marked out as a badminton court. Faded white lines lay along the scuffed floor. Frank, Gareth and Bet stood behind Suzanne; like courtiers, thought Stephen. Alana remained impassive but her eyes roamed around the faces, taking in all the details.

Rory sauntered in, a smug look on his face and sidled up to the wall opposite Stephen. People moved out of his way while his sidekicks Deek and Tim took up a place either side of him. No-one spoke much, fearful of what Morgan wanted. Finally, the Colonel arrived.

Boot steps could be heard in the entranceway. Morgan entered first, followed by his Captain and Lieutenant. Both junior officers carried rifles, held across them with the muzzles angled down. Their index fingers rested outside the trigger guard while their gloved hands held the grip. Removing his beret, Morgan smiled at Suzanne. When he spoke, a soft Welsh accent filled the room.

"Good morning, everyone. Thank you for coming." He sounded grateful, but everyone here had felt ordered to be there. All could see the silver pistols at his hip. "I am very happy to tell you we intend to winter here."

Some people to Stephen's left shuffled their feet. One of the men, Charlie, caught Stephen's eye. Morgan continued on with his speech about how everyone should make them welcome. He leaned on his silver pistols. Charlie turned back to listen. Alana had noticed this and she exchanged a look with Stephen.

Morgan asked if anyone had any questions. There was silence for a moment before Suzanne stood up. Composing herself first, she asked, a tremor in her voice, "And how do you intend to feed yourselves?"

Morgan smiled. Captain Weaver glanced at the Lieutenant, who swallowed. Morgan said evenly, "We will be availing ourselves of your hospitality." His eyes roamed around the group to allow them time to digest his point.

"Colonel Morgan, we will barely feed ourselves this winter." Suzanne had spoken respectfully but firmly. Frank rearranged his feet and moved closer to Suzanne, though his grey beard jittered at his mouth.

Morgan smiled again. He replaced his beret carefully before opening his hands. "I'll leave you to work out the details." He turned on his heels, followed by his officers.

Rory and his friends skulked out while the meeting broke up into angry denunciations of how that was handled by Suzanne and how they would cope. Charlie nodded to his brother, Vincent, and the two of them went to go. As he passed Stephen, Charlie said, "Time to move on, I think."

Stephen held him by the arm. "Where will you go?"

Charlie shook his head and shrugged. He followed Vincent out the room. While the shouting went on, Stephen said to Alana, "What did you make of that?"

She thought for a minute, looked around, and then pulled Stephen to the side. They moved away from the others, who were moving into the middle of the room, where Suzanne appealed for calm. Alana said, "Take out Morgan? Weaver takes his place. Lieutenant Baxter is ineffectual, probably incompetent."

Stephen felt shocked at her assessment. He looked at the crowd, then back to her. "So what we do with Weaver and Baxter?"

"How the hell should I know?" She suddenly seemed frustrated at him. "Just remember those things."

He nodded, bewildered by her sudden insistence. He

motioned for them to go and the three of them left. Karen held onto Alana's hand, having been quiet the whole time.

When they stepped outside, they crossed the road to go over to the wash-house. Stephen looked left towards the cattle-grid. Rory was talking with Morgan while Deek and Tim held back at the corner of the hall. Rory was pointing towards the direction of the wash-houses while Morgan listened intently. Stephen kept them moving, but slowly, so he could see what was happening. He was horrified to witness Morgan hand Rory one of the army rifles.

"Shit," Stephen growled. He pulled the girls round the corner to where they would be unobserved. "Listen to me-"

"Did he just-?" Alana had seen what took place and was outraged but she kept her voice down.

"Just listen," said Stephen. He was panicked and he spoke impulsively, not having consulted Gary, but he knew he had to speak. "Between Duns and Chirnside, there is an old petrol station with a burnt-out tanker in the forecourt. Half a kilometre east is the road to Edrom. At the end of that road is a brick house with red-painted window frames. The house is gutted but in the back garden is an honest to god cold-war bunker. The entrance is too out in the open while these soldiers are out and about but if they're here, well..."

Alana gulped. She searched his face. She knew what he was telling her, that the bunker was stocked with tins. She also knew what was about to happen, they both did. A squad of soldiers double-timed round the corner and headed for the wash-houses.

16

RORY HAD SOLD them out. They sat in Gary's place amongst the remains of their gear. Phil rested wrists on his knees and leaned against the wall, next to a great hole. Gary hung his head and stared into the void. He had dug the hole in the plasterboard himself. Stephen had had the idea of lifting the floorboards. Inside they had stashed all their stuff and stacked wood up in front to conceal everything.

It was all gone, stolen by Morgan's Unit. The prized shotgun was in Deek's hands, while Tim was in possession of Stephen's Glock. Everything else had been pillaged by the soldiers; their food, everything. All they were left with was the clothes they stood up in.

Stephen knew, though he said nothing, that Alana still had her Glock concealed on her person. She played with Karen's hair as the girl dozed in her lap. Stephen rested his forehead on clasped hands. The sight of Rory being handed the rifle boiled his blood but he held his rage down. He let it simmer inside him. He'd taken a punch when he had tried to intervene. Two SA80s pointed at their heads had halted further protests from him and Gary.

Suzanne and the rest of them had watched from a distance and done nothing. What could they do, he told himself, though he still found himself angry at their inaction. They were weak, defenceless and afraid, but he couldn't help but think there were a few smug looks. He knew he was resented for having tins of food while they toiled in their gardens. Not everyone appreciated trading with him and would have taken pleasure in seeing it taken from him.

Clipped sounds of hooves on tarmac sounded from outside. Alana was first to the window. Phil followed Gary's lead of staying where they were and not moving at all. Stephen asked, "What's going on?"

"They're pulling out." Alana kept her tone even,

reporting the facts. Karen joined her and tip-toed to see. "Two are staying at the manse. The rest are headed up to the forest."

Stephen dragged himself up and peered out the window. "All our food is in the manse. They've left two guards."

Out in the street, Morgan led the way as they rode round the cattle grid and headed up the grassy path. The two Privates left behind disappeared inside the Manse and closed the door.

"What are you thinking?" Alana asked.

"I'm going in there to get my stuff." Stephen was serious.

"It won't be easy."

"It will be impossible," Gary said. He stayed where he was.

Alana took Stephen by the arm. "Let's just think about it first."

"What's there to think about? I'll chap the door, you blow their heads off with the Glock and we'll get our stuff back."

"There's a way to do these things." Alana was insistent. She was thinking about something, calculating again. She gripped his arm tighter, holding him close. "I was a Forensic Psychologist at Fettes."

She had his full attention. Sharing something about herself was something he had thought she would not do. Near the famous public school of the same name in Edinburgh, Fettes was the HQ of Lothian and Borders Police.

Gary shifted round to see. "You're Police?"

Alana nodded at the question but kept her attention on Stephen. "When everything turned to shit I got assigned to an Armed Unit. This police issue Glock 26 was what I trained on." She patted her hip.

"What are you saying?" Stephen knew she was trusting him completely. Maybe it was because he had shared the location of the bunker and maybe it was something else but she had an idea about something. Stephen decided he would figure out her motivation later.

"I'm saying you walked into that farmhouse and pulled us out of there, but it may not happen like that again." Alana let him think about that for a moment then released his arm.

A rifle shot sounded outside.

17

STEPHEN WAS FIRST out, followed by Gary and Phil. Alana hung back inside. At the end of their path, next to the wall, Rory had shot a round into the air from his new rifle. He was grinning. Deek and Tim giggled to each other.

"How do like that?" Rory shouted. He fired again. Deek and Tim ducked momentarily, in shock at the noise, but laughed it up once the sound drifted away.

Stephen walked towards Rory and was not put off by him leveling the rifle. "Why don't you fuck off, Rory?" He felt Gary and Phil's presence behind him.

Nothing changed on Rory's expression. Triumphantly, he laughed, his head rocking back. At that, Stephen rushed up and smacked him right in the teeth. He heard Alana pull back the slide on the Glock. She must have come outside, thought Stephen. Rubbing his mouth, Rory was shocked but he quickly gained his composure and went to raise his weapon.

"Stop it right now!" The shout, from a woman's voice, was from the street to Stephen's right. Her tone caught Rory off-balance and he stopped his movement. It was Suzanne. She was striding towards them, a few people behind her. "I mean it," she said, her teeth bared and her eyes wide. "Stop it right now." She roared the last word and came right up to them. It emboldened others who crowded around. Not all seemed to be with Suzanne, Stephen suddenly thought, and he backed off slightly.

Rory sneered right in Suzanne's face. "Who do you think you are, Suzanne?"

Stephen used the same tone but less angry. "Back off, Rory. You sold us out you son of a bitch."

"What of it?" Rory made some room to swing the rifle about. A few quailed but some others held their ground, staring at Stephen.

"That's enough, Rory." Suzanne tried to put her hand

on Rory's arm but he flinched away before pushing the rifle into her chest with both hands. Suzanne dropped like a stone right onto the tarmac.

Bodies pressed forward. Rory gripped the rifle under his armpit and lifted his head. "This what you want? This it?"

Stephen felt the situation going out of control. He tried to move but the press of bodies around him had cut off his escape. He looked to Gary but he was engaged in pulling someone off Phil. He looked back to Suzanne, who was on the ground but being helped up. Rory dug the muzzle into Stephen's ribs. Stephen looked to Alana. She was raising the pistol in the air, apparently ready to shoot.

Stephen looked behind her. "Alana!" he yelled and pointed behind her. Her arm recoiled and she twisted round. The two soldiers, left behind by Morgan, were closing in on her. She tried to react but they were on her. One punched her on the cheek and she stumbled. The pistol fell away from her hand.

Gary had two men on him. Phil had pulled himself away. Someone punched Stephen on the back of the head. It was Tim, now taunting him, as Rory poked the muzzle at Stephen's body.

The pistol hit the ground and the soldiers had overwhelmed Alana. Someone grabbed Stephen's body and stopped him moving forward. Phil saw the pistol on the ground. Deek slapped Stephen on the head. Stephen pushed him back but it provoked the others into punching him. He tried to move.

The soldiers had grabbed Alana and were dragging her away. She screamed and reached out towards Stephen. Someone punched Stephen in the gut and he folded. Phil grabbed the pistol from the floor at the same time as someone else. He wrestled it away. He looked at it in his hand. He pointed it unconvincingly at the crowd, who baulked, giving Phil space to turn and run away.

Stephen saw Gary go down and he felt punches on his

head and on his back as he fell to the ground.

18

"SHAME YOU'LL MISS the party, lads."

Paul looked in the service hatch of the cell door, his smirk evident. He lifted the hatch and locked it from the outside. His steps went back down the hall and they could hear his voice mix in with others in the Police Station.

Stephen sighed. Locked in a police cell, he looked up at the window, a high up panel of diffused light. It was late afternoon. Gary sat opposite patting a burst lower lip. Gary put his foot on the concrete slab which passed for a bed.

"Party?" Gary said.

"I don't want to even think about that," Stephen responded, genuinely meaning it.

"What do you think will happen to us?" Gary sounded afraid. It was dark now and he was little more than a vague shape to Stephen's eyes. He sat curled up on the bed.

"I would have killed us by now."

Stephen heard Gary whimper. He thought about Ellen and Jack and wondered how he had managed to become responsible for other people again.

"He ran off," said Gary. "I thought he was a mate."

"Yeah," was all Stephen could manage to discuss Phil.

Something popped. It woke him up. Stephen was hugging himself in the cold. Some sounds from the police station outside their cell.

"Gaz." Stephen slapped Gary on his curled up leg. Gary jumped awake.

Keys jangled and someone shuffled in the hall outside the cell. The door opened. A blaze of light from the hallway but Stephen could make out Paul. He readied himself to rise and rush to door.

"Stephen, it's me. It's Phil." Someone pushed Paul forward and he landed at Stephen's feet.

"It is Phil," Gary said, recognising the boy first. Phil stood in the doorway, grinning. The Glock was in his hand. He waved at them with his other hand for them to follow him.

19

OUT IN THE old public area of the police station Stephen found Frank pointing a garden fork at the back of a man on his knees. Frank grinned. "You alright, fella?"

"I'm fine, thanks. Who's this?" Stephen walked round to take look at a face of the person on his knees. Stephen knew the face but not his name.

"His name's Dave. One of Rory's friends." Frank was scathing and he pushed the points of the fork into Dave's head.

Dave flinched and he looked really scared. Stephen just looked at him. He heard Phil and Gary dragging Paul back through. They threw him to the floor next to Dave. Paul glared at Stephen; blood trickled down the side of his head.

"Did my friend shoot you?" Stephen asked, with exaggerated sympathy and looked up at Phil, who shrugged apologetically.

"He tried to," said Paul, unrepentant and angry. "This is a splinter off the counter."

Stephen laughed. "But it made you think twice didn't it?" He straightened up and clapped Phil on the arm. The boy smiled but reddened. Gary grinned and punched Phil on the arm.

Stephen composed himself. "Right, so what's going on? Alana and Karen?"

Frank lowered his head. Phil reddened further. "I came for you first."

"You did well, Phil." Stephen walked over to Phil and placed his hands on his shoulder. Phil looked like he was about to cry. "We'll go and get them now."

"You'll have no chance," Paul spat, still kneeling on the floor.

"Do tell," said Stephen. He took the fork off Frank and leaned it on Paul's shoulders.

Paul paused but, so angry at having been overpowered,

he couldn't help himself. "Your girls are over at the hall. Rory's opened the warehouses and after they've had a party, they're going to have another party."

Stephen breathed in but he felt dizzy. The thought of it paralysed him. He tried to catch himself to stop himself thinking about their whisky and their plans. He looked about him. He pressed the fork into Paul's shoulders but somehow held himself back.

"Shall we lock them up?" Gary said. He had stepped up close to Stephen sensing his friend's change of mood. Stephen came to a decision. He looked Gary in the eye. Gary nodded and backed off.

Stephen leaned forward and spoke into Paul's ear. "Well, Paul? Are you with me or against me?"

Paul tutted. "Fuck off, Stephen."

It was his last thought. Stephen drove the fork into the back of Paul's neck. It broke the skin as Paul fell away. Stephen pressed the handle and pushed forward. Dave screamed and scuttled off to the side. Phil stepped in and pointed the Glock right at Dave's head. That stopped him screaming. Paul's body shuddered and died, the last Policeman of the village.

"Christ, Stephen," said Frank, a disgusted look on his face.

Stephen put his boot onto Paul's head and withdrew the fork. He turned to their other prisoner. "What about you, Dave?"

"I'm with you, with you," he blurted and tried to squirm away.

Stephen closed in on him and held the bloodied end of the fork up to Dave's face. "Listen to me very carefully. We are going to win tonight. In the morning, we are going to run this place. Do you understand?"

Dave nodded. He had become still as he listened to Stephen.

"Nothing you do could stop us. If you tried something,

like raise the alarm, it won't make a difference. It just means that in the morning, I'll be looking for you."

Stephen let Dave think about that for a moment. He felt exhilarated at the power of the four of them in this room against two men. At that thought, he softened, "Do you have a weapon?"

Dave looked perplexed, like he hadn't understood the question. Phil pressed the gun into his head and said, "Do you have a weapon?" Dave shook his head.

Stephen straightened. "Get him on his feet."

Gary and Frank pulled Dave to his feet. Stephen motioned for Phil to lower the Glock. He hefted the fork in both hands and said to Dave, "Get to the wash-houses. Relieve whoever is guarding the girls, give them some story, and then make sure no-one takes them out of there. Got it?"

Dave gulped and nodded, looking to the three men. Stephen handed the fork back to Frank. "Keep an eye on him and back him up when he gets there."

Frank nodded. He looked pale. "Come on, son." He slapped Dave on the shoulder with the back of his hand. Dave smoothed his clothes and breathed out. He attempted a humble smile as he left.

"He looks grateful," said Phil.

"He should be." Stephen glanced down at Paul. He walked over to the raised counter PC Paul would have used to greet the public in an earlier life. He noticed a small chunk cut out by Phil's shot.

"I've got to ask," Gary said to Phil. "Why didn't you fire the gun when you picked it up?"

Phil held the pistol in his hand before handing it to Gary. "I didn't know how." Gary unclipped the magazine and checked the number of shots he had.

Stephen fingered the hole in the counter. "It seems you still don't."

Gary and Stephen shared a quick subdued laugh. "How

do we do this?" asked Phil, trying to change the subject.

Stephen held his hands out. He looked at the counter. There was a broad shelf underneath but it was empty. Just under the counter was a broad drawer with a half-oval copper handle. He pulled the drawer open and smiled. "Paul was holding out on us." He pulled out another police-issue Glock and handed it to Phil. Gary showed him how to unhook the magazine.

"And one for the road." Stephen pulled out a three-quarter full bottle of whisky. He went to put it to his lips then thought better of it. "Ready?"

Gary's blood was up. "Let's do it, man."

Phil palmed the magazine back in and held the barrel, offering the grip to Stephen.

"That's yours now, Phil," said Stephen. "You earned it."

Phil grinned and Gary slapped him hard on the back. He nearly toppled.

20

THERE WAS A party going on in the hall. Laughter and chatter could be heard from across the village. The rest of the place was quiet. The houses at the back were dark. Stephen wondered how many were at the party. They moved quickly through the high street, keeping to the side of the buildings and their sound to a minimum. Having decided a detour through the distillery down below might have been safer, but slower, they made their way directly to the hall.

Noisy shouting inside masked their sounds. Candles burning inside flickered shadows on the curtains. As agreed, Phil peeled off and headed for the wash-houses. Gary followed Stephen run passed the hall, and round the church, towards the manse. The former minister's home was dark and Stephen wondered if the soldiers were in the hall.

Creeping up to the windows, they looked inside but could see nothing because of the gloom. Gary quietly tried the door but it was locked. Stephen cursed silently. He wanted whatever weapons might be in there but dared not break a window. He tapped Gary on the shoulder and they ran back to the hall.

They dropped to the ground when someone came outside. Followed by a woman, the man walked on rubber legs back towards the village proper. The woman leaned against him, just as drunk. Unnoticed by the couple, Stephen and Gary let them go, before moving again. Phil ran up to them at the spot near the main door. He was carrying a brick in one hand and a glowing piece of wood in the other. He had taken it from the fireplace in the wash-house.

Stephen whispered, "Everything okay?"

"Yeah," whispered Phil between gulps of air. "The girls are fine and Dave and Frank are there."

Stephen nodded. Their eyes had adjusted to the dark and the small light glowing from the ember. He said, "Rory, Deek and Tim; those two soldiers. Everyone else can go."

Gary and Phil breathed agreement. Phil pushed the Glock into Stephen's hand, "You'll do better with this."

Stephen took it gratefully. "I'll give you the honour of this, then." He handed Phil the bottle he had found in the police station, which now had a rag of Paul's shirt in it, soaked in whisky.

Phil handled the bottle carefully. He touched the rag to the ember and blew on it to catch. It flared and they had to squint and look away. Phil whirled round, holding the bottle to his side. He ran up to the window furthest from the door and bricked the window. Shouts died inside as the glass shattered and fell inwards. In one fluid movement, Phil launched the bottle in through the gap and span away.

A crash of broken glass as the bottle hit the floor inside and a massive flare as the whisky caught fire. The curtains were the first to catch it and the shouting started again.

First out the door were a couple of women followed by one of the soldiers. Stephen and Gary had positioned themselves on one knee. Stephen took aim and fired. The soldier ducked but he was unharmed and, crucially, unarmed too. People came running out and jostled the soldier. Gary fired and the soldier's head jerked back and he fell to the ground. A woman screamed and ran off towards the cattle grid as if to flee the village altogether.

Amongst the mass of people, Stephen made out the other soldier staggering out, unable to comprehend what was happening. Unable to get a clear shot, Stephen stood and walked forward. Up close, the soldier saw him and fear shook his face. Stephen shot him in the mouth.

Glass tinkled onto the road. Shots sounded. Someone, Rory, had poked his rifle out the window and was firing into the air. Gary shot at the window but it bounced off the stone frame. Rory shot again and one of the partygoers, whisky bottle in hand, fell over. As he landed, Phil plucked the bottle out of his hand and threw it in the window Rory was firing from. The bottle smashed and another flare of light. Phil had another brick in his hand and slammed it into someone else's head.

As the people thinned, coughing out into the street. Stephen pushed people aside and grabbed them to see their faces. He could see Gary struggling with someone onto the ground. A crack and something bounced off the pavement spinning some tarmac past Stephen's legs.

Rushing outside, firing wildly, Rory suddenly ran out of rounds. His face was shocked as he reached Stephen, his finger clicking the trigger uselessly. Stephen grinned and punched him square in the face.

21

RORY KNEELED ON the road; hands clasped on the back of his head. Blood filled his teeth. He spat it onto the ground in front of Stephen. At either side of him, in the same position, were his friends. Tim looked woozy from a brick on the side of his head from Phil. Deek just look shame-faced, and scared, despite his tussle with Gary. Their faces were lit up by the hall burning. In front of them, the contents of their pockets had been emptied onto the ground. Amongst the grubby debris shone the keys to the warehouses. Stephen smiled at Rory as he fished them off the ground and slipped them in his own pocket. Rory held Stephen's gaze.

Gary was looking at Rory's rifle. "It's the cadet version. I used this in the cadets."

Stephen shook his head at Rory. "You sold us out for a cadet rifle?"

Gary sneered, "Not even a grown up rifle."

"And not many rounds either," said Phil, who had his Glock back and pointed it at the three kneeling men.

Stephen stared at Rory, who had that odd sneer on his face; the same one he'd had the other day. He thought for a moment, "Watch them for a minute. No-one moves."

Gary nodded and threw the cadet rifle to the ground. He pulled Stephen's Glock which had been retrieved from Tim.

Stephen went off to the wash-houses. Frank and Dave stood around nervously outside. He put a hand on each of their shoulders. "Good lads. Off you go home." Frank and Dave looked at each other. Frank nodded and tapped the younger man on the arm to leave.

Stephen watched them go then went inside to his billet. Alana shivered when the door opened. She sat on the mattress, hugging Karen. She breathed out a few times, gently unhooked herself from Karen, stood, and rushed towards him. She embraced him and they wrapped their arms round each other. She held onto him tightly.

"Thank God," she said. "Thank God."

Stephen pulled himself back. "We don't have much time. The fire might have been seen by Morgan."

She nodded once, relief making her breathe quickly.

He continued, "Go to the manse. Secure whatever is there. Guns, ammo..." Stephen searched for the words.

"Our food." Alana finished.

He took her hand and she motioned for Karen to follow. The girl jumped up and grabbed Alana's other hand. The three of them stepped outside and walked round to the hall. Stephen had to hold Alana back because she started shouting at the men, cursing them and clearly wanting to get at them. She kicked out but Stephen got a hold of her, reminding her, "The manse."

Alana calmed herself. She snatched Karen's hand back and they made off to the manse behind the hall which blazed in the night. Stephen walked up to Phil and took the pistol out his hand.

"Go and help Alana," he said gently. "We'll take care of this."

Phil nodded once to Stephen and scurried off after the girls. Stephen turned to Rory. "Get on your feet."

Rory spat again, but he got to his feet. Deek followed but Tim vomited. Stephen instructed them to help him. Rory and Deek grabbed an arm each and got him up. "Move it," said Stephen and motioned towards the cattle-grid.

Rory sneered again but he turned and pulled Tim. Deek followed meekly. Stephen looked to Gary, who stared at the back of the three men's heads. They rounded the cattle-grid. Stephen looked up at the manse. In the firelight, he saw Alana on the doorstep. Phil had broken the lock and had entered. She watched them for a moment before following Phil inside.

An hour later, Stephen and Gary returned to the manse. In an expansive front room, Alana had lit a fire and she sat next to it in a big chair with one the soldier's rifles over her lap. She had seen it was them and was relaxed when they entered. She didn't say anything. Karen lay sleeping in the corner on a ratty old sofa, snuggled up in the blankets from the wash-house.

Stephen felt exhausted. He rubbed Gary's shoulder as he closed the door behind him. Phil stood at the top of the stairs. Gary followed him up, dog-tired.

Alana looked at Stephen then rocked her head back into the room. She took his hand and they went passed the staircase to a kitchen. Their cans were stacked neatly up next to the back door. Alana eased herself onto the work surface and took off her top. Stephen held her close, breathing in the smell of her hair.

22

BOOTS CLATTERED ON the staircase. Stephen breathed awake. Alana did the same. It was light. Gary blundered towards the front door, stopped and looked in the front room. Alana lay, wrapped in a blanket, across Stephen's knees as they curled up together on the big chair.

Gary grinned. "Nice." Then he was off out the front door after Phil, who had already gone outside unheard.

Alana sat up and looked around, bleary-eyed. Karen stood at the window, already out of her sofa bed, looking outside. Alana pulled herself up and shuffled over to Karen. She kept the blanket over her shoulders, despite having dressed again before sleep. Stephen suddenly felt cold. He saw the fire was out.

"Morning, sweetie," Alana said as she knelt down and shared her blanket with Karen. She looked out the window. "They're like boys with a new toy."

Stephen sniffed and blew the air out his cheeks. He jumped up and left the room. Stepping outside, he saw that Phil had a rifle up to his cheek and Gary was showing him the ropes. Liberated from the dead soldiers, their two rifles were prized and useful weapons. Stephen rubbed the back of his head and breathed in cold morning air. Stale smoke drifted over from the village hall. He heard sounds of someone rooting about inside the ruined building.

He left the boys to what they were doing and walked round the blackened building. At the front, Frank and Dave were dragging the body of one of the soldiers. They pulled him over to an old car trailer where the body of the other already lay draped over the back. Stephen went over to help them.

As he neared, he saw the body of Paul lying next to the first soldier. He gulped and looked around. It was early and there was no-one about. He greeted Frank and Dave and assisted them lifting the soldier onto the cart. He was heavy and the dead weight was difficult, even with the three of them doing the lifting.

"Thanks, Frank. Dave." Stephen said. He clapped his hands together and rubbed them.

Frank sighed. "We couldn't leave them. Especially not Paul."

"Yeah." Stephen looked away.

"He was a good village bobby once," said Frank. "A long time ago."

Stephen fought down the urge to tell Frank that Paul should have stayed that way and intervened on their behalf the night before but he knew the older man was also trying to tell him something else. Paul might have been a good policeman once, but this new world required a new police force. Paul hadn't cut it.

"What will we do with them?" Dave looked ill as he waved a finger at the corpses.

"We'll bury them in the churchyard, lad," said Frank.

Stephen looked at Dave's shoes, just battered and dirty trainers. He looked at the boots on the soldiers. "These boots fit you, Dave?"

Dave curled his lip in disgust as he looked at the dead men's feet. "Probably, but..."

"We'll sort you out, lad," said Frank. He looked at Stephen. "We'll get this, you've got visitors." He cocked a head behind him.

Stephen looked up the street and saw a thin line of people walking their way. He helped Frank and Dave get the trailer moving towards the church. As they moved, Stephen kept looking over his shoulder as the people came nearer. When the trailer had cleared the hall, Stephen called to Phil and Gary.

They came running down but Stephen ushered them back. Gary took the rifle off Phil and he slung it across himself the way the soldiers did. The three of them backed up to the house.

As the people came nearer, Stephen could see they wore thin smiles. They looked humble and were carrying some things. Bet was first up. She carried a small bundle of clothes. She handed them to Stephen. He saw a small pink jumper and a small pair of jeans amongst some other things; a girl's clothes. He looked in the window at Alana's puzzled expression staring out.

Next up was Iqbal. He carried Gary's shotgun and the small box of shells. "From Rory's place," he said, handing it over to Phil.

Alana came out the door and stood next to Stephen, taking the bundle off him and showing them to Karen, who appeared beside her legs.

There were a few other gifts; blankets, pillows, some clothes for Alana. Most of the village was there, looking at them. Stephen said, "Thank you for this."

Gareth stepped forward, and moved towards the gate to take up his usual position on top. "Don't thank us, Stephen. Just make the trains run on time."

Stephen knew what that meant. He was in charge now. After all, he had told Dave the night before that in the morning he would be running things. He breathed in. "Where's Suzanne?"

"Won't come out," said Bet. "After she got thumped, she's locked herself in."

Stephen thought for a minute. He felt the weight of it on him, suddenly, but he knew what to do. "Gareth? You keep an eye out for Morgan. Ring that bell as soon as you see them."

Gareth gave a thumbs up. Stephen looked out at everyone. "We'll meet in the church tonight. Everyone."

"What about the kids?" someone shouted.

"Everyone." Stephen saw a few people nod though a few shook their heads quietly to each other. "Agreed?"

"Stephen?" It was Gareth from atop the gate.

Stephen stepped forward. "Morgan? Already?"

Gareth laughed. "No, something you won't believe. Sails." He pointed out to sea and everyone's eyes followed. Sure enough, out on the horizon was a small pale sail. A boat was heading their way, the first for a number of years.

23

STEPHEN AND GARY stood at the end of the pier.
They held back from the moorings where Phil stood
watching a large yacht approach. Margaretvale bay formed a
natural horseshoe shaped harbour and the yacht sailed into
calm waters. Two crew members lowered the sails and one
of them dropped an anchor as the boat stopped. Still some
distance from the pier, the two men organised themselves
on board. A small wooden boat, tethered to the stern,
bobbed up and down.

One of the crew members lifted some sort of rifle in the
air, one handed, indicating he had it but not using it, while
his companion watched the pier through binoculars. Gary
readied his rifle, the army issue SA80. Stephen could see he
was enjoying owning it. Before running down, Stephen had
divvied up the guns between his party. Gary had his
shotgun so Alana got her Glock back and so on. Stephen
kept his Glock in the waistband of his trousers. His Lugar
monocular was still missing, having been taken during "the
arrest", so they just had to watch.

On the boat, the crew member was making an elaborate
show of putting the rifle onto the deck and stepping back
from it. The other man lowered the binoculars and shouted,
"Ahoy! We just need some fresh water."

Stephen looked at Gary, who shrugged. He was aware of
the crowd who hung back near the distillery gates, watching
his every move. Stephen raised an arm and beckoned the
men in. The one with the binoculars made his way to the
small boat. When he jumped in, his partner untied it and he
started rowing to the pier. The partner stayed on the yacht.

When he was near the pier, the man stopped rowing. He
said, "We don't want trouble. Just fresh water."

"We won't offer you trouble, mister," said Gary. He
stressed the word "offer" and the man in the boat showed
he knew what Gary meant by nodding wryly. He threw Phil

a rope, which Phil caught after a fumble and pulled the boat in. He made an attempt at tying it up. The man stepped ashore. On the wooden mooring, he stumbled a bit.

"Just finding my legs," he said. He turned to the yacht and raised four fingers in the air, some kind of signal. Turning back, he said, "I'm Malcolm." He held a hand out and smiled, friendly enough.

"Stephen." He shook Malcolm's hand, but he never introduced Gary or Phil. They remained quiet.

"We just need water, said Malcolm. "If we could maybe just go to the burn."

Using the Scottish term for a stream, Malcolm pointed at the mouth of the River Margaretvale. It was the source of water for the village and had been dammed higher up the hill to make a reservoir. Only the overflow found its way to the sea. Stephen couldn't see any reason why they couldn't have water. His eye caught the creels sitting quietly at the moorings and thought of Frank fishing.

"We'll be on our way after that," said Malcolm. "Maybe you could spare some whisky too?"

Stephen looked up at the long warehouse painted with "Glen Craobhmore". Turning back to Malcolm, he said, "I'll tell you what. We'll fill your tank. We still have water from the mains. In return, give us some news."

Malcolm gave a shallow nod, like he was thinking. "And the whisky?"

"Go and do some fishing for us. Take those creels too and get us some shell fish. Bring back as much as you can by tonight and we'll trade you a fair price in whisky."

Malcolm gave that shallow nod again and a sly smile appeared on his face. "Fair enough."

They shook on it. Stephen suspected Malcolm had thought he could maybe have gotten the whisky and water for nothing and be on their way. He sent Phil up the pier to organise the water. Malcolm signalled his companion on the yacht, by holding up a fist, and soon it was berthed up against the moorings.

Frank operated the hoses, installed at an earlier time for tourist yachts, and filled the water tanks of Malcolm's boat. All the time, Malcolm spoke openly about what they had seen. "Some places like yours up and down the coast, but nothing big, though we steered clear of Edinburgh itself. We're headed south to see what we can find." He described fires, lighting up the sky, which they had seen when they had been off the north-east coast, and what may have been other vessels, hazily glimpsed on the horizon.

"This is the first boat we've seen for a long time," said Stephen. Alana and Karen had joined him and they admired its faded white hull. Neat script lettering at the bow said it was called "The Mercury".

"We were lucky," said Malcolm. He gestured to his friend whom he hadn't introduced by name. "We found her berthed at Largs."

"You've been all round the north?" Alana said, incredulous at The Mercury's journey from Largs on the west coast to here on the east.

Malcolm smiled and nodded. "We were lucky." He stepped aboard. Phil ran to untie The Mercury from its mooring. Malcolm's companion used a boat hook to push away while Malcolm raised a sail. "We'll be back for that whisky."

"We'll be here," Stephen called out. As the yacht slipped out, he turned his back and said to Alana, "What do you make of that?"

She leaned in. "He never introduced his friend."

Stephen shrugged his eyebrows. "I never introduced you or the boys."

"And he's not telling you how he found the boat. One boat left moored up? When all the others were already away or burnt out? You've seen Berwick, I'm sure."

Stephen agreed with her, remembering the sight she was

describing. He gathered Phil and Gary together. "Keep your wits about you when they get back."

Gary and Phil grinned at each other, eager for adventure.

24

IN THE END, The Mercury brought back crabs, a lobster, and a heap of fish. Having liberated the warehouse keys from Rory the night before, Stephen gave the sailors a small barrel of whisky which Malcolm and his mate seemed happy with. Despite the failing light, The Mercury sailed off to the South, rounding the point, and disappeared from view. There were gaps in the warehouse but there were still countless barrels of whisky. Stephen hoped they could use it to trade with other passers-by. Perhaps things were returning to normal, he thought.

In the church, Stephen shared out the fish amongst eager villagers. The dank atmosphere of the church was replaced first by the fresh salty smell of fish and then by cooking. Charlie and Vincent had lit a fire in a pit in the middle of the church which in earlier times would have been used to heat the congregation.

It was a relaxed atmosphere, with everyone enjoying themselves. Happy chatter about The Mercury and its news; the fires to the north-east; other villages; some ships on the horizon. Whilst some were still eating, Stephen stood up. "Most of you know me. I am Stephen." He introduced Alana, Karen, Gary and Phil. Then he was stuck for words. He looked to Alana who gave him a brief warm smile. "We need to run things better round here. There are to be no more robberies. We trade things. And the whisky and the water belong to us all."

There were a few murmurs of approval. Charlie spoke up, "We need to control the warehouses carefully. If we can get fish for whisky..." He let the thought hang in the air.

Frank said, "We need our own boat."

There were agreements to that and conversations sprang up. Stephen quietened them down and said, "And the women here are to go unmolested." He instantly regretted the use of the word though he had used it deliberately. He followed it by saying quietly, "Or you answer to me."

Everyone went silent. He had basically threatened them and asserted his authority over them. After a moment, Alana prompted him, "How will we organise ourselves?" This perked everyone's interest.

"We'll have a council. Four members to make decisions instead of one. Voted in to office by us all." Stephen was referring to Suzanne, who had stayed at home, and had run things in the past with barely any consultation, let alone consensus.

Charlie said, "What about two judges? Separate from the council, where we can take disputes to."

Stephen looked to Alana. With her eyes, she agreed with the idea. She played with Karen's hair. Stephen said, "Great idea. Any other ideas?"

"Yes," said Gareth, emphatically. "What about Morgan?"

Stephen beckoned Phil and Gary to his side. He put an arm on each of their shoulders. "I'll take care of that."

25

"THERE'S SOMETHING ELSE everyone's too afraid to ask."

Stephen looked Charlie right in the eye when he said that. They had been discussing Morgan. Loose tongues, due to whisky, had confided in Charlie late at night. Some soldiers had told him the unit had kept their discipline through Morgan but were long ago cut off from any chain of command. Charlie shared this with Stephen.

Stephen stood at a makeshift paddock the soldiers had created next to the manse. Two horses, previously owned by the dead soldiers, had trotted over to see them. Stephen had promised the horses to Alana and Karen, hoping they would not have to be slaughtered for food. Alana showed Karen how to feed the first horse with an apple. Dressed in her new clothes, and pair of just too big trainers, Karen followed her movements and the second horse snaffled the apple out her hand to the girl's obvious delight. The sun was shining, probably the last of the autumn warmth.

"So what's this thing, people are too afraid to ask?" Stephen spoke gently but directly.

Charlie cleared his throat. "We need, we need another constable." He tried a nervous smile. "I'm glad Paul's gone." Charlie glanced at three fresh graves in the church yard.

Stephen glanced at Alana. She gave a short noncommittal shake of her head, unseen by Charlie. Stephen said to the man, "You want the job?"

"Not at all," Charlie said squarely. "I want on the council."

"Good luck on the vote," said Stephen, then he sighed. "I'll think about it. Until then..."

Charlie nodded. He knew what Stephen meant. Until there was a constable, Stephen would be the law and order. Charlie waved them goodbye. He ruffled Karen's hair. She pulled back, disgusted, and Stephen thought Alana was going to hit him.

When he had gone, Stephen turned his attention to the horses, but spoke to Alana. "You don't fancy it? Constable?"

She laughed. "Chief Constable, maybe."

He smiled. They had spent the night together again and he had enjoyed every minute. She looked him in the eye, a wicked glint shone out.

From on top of his junkyard gate, Gareth started ringing his bell.

26

MORGAN'S UNIT OF ten rode into the village. Morgan sat up on his horse like he had a steel rod in his back. The others looked exhausted. Chin straps had already been unclipped. Two of the men walked, pulling their horses, each with a deer strapped over the saddle. Every one of them was grubby, in contrast to their normal well turned out selves.

Morgan stepped down from his horse and handed the reins to Lieutenant Baxter. Weaver held back and stayed on his horse outside the cattle-grid, as if sniffing the air, which still had the stale smell of charred wood from the ruined hall. He was looking around as the rest of the unit lifted themselves off the horses and threw down their helmets. A few fell onto the grass and lay back in the sunlight. Gareth quietly climbed down from on top of the gate.

Weaver shouted out towards the manse, "Pilrig. Jones." No response from the soldiers they had left behind. Weaver seemed troubled. He caught sight of three fresh graves in the cemetery. "Colonel Morgan?" he called out, alarm in his voice.

Morgan turned. He was on the path to the manse. Silver pistols shone in the sunlight. A few of the men sat up at Weaver's tone. Morgan's eyes blazed. There was a massive crack. Morgan's head exploded and his teal beret flew into the air. He dropped to his knees. Soldiers dived for their weapons.

"Cease fire! Cease fire!"

Weaver's horse spun round. He had a pistol out and was trying to see, yelling, "Who gave that order?"

Stephen emerged from his hiding place within the gate. "Cease fire!" he shouted. He had the shotgun in his right hand. He grabbed the horse's bridle with his left and jammed the shotgun into Weaver's neck. As Weaver aimed at Stephen, the shotgun was fired. Weaver fell back and

Stephen let go of the horse. Shots crackled around as Stephen ducked back to the gate. More shots were fired from the manse and from inside the burnt-out village hall.

Stephen shouted again, "Cease fire!" He fired the other barrel into the air. The shotgun made a loud boom and the soldiers went quiet. They had been caught unawares and were at a loss to know what to do. Stephen emerged, having left the shotgun behind. He had the pistol in his hand. "Cease fire!"

Gary came out of the Manse, his rifle at the ready. Phil emerged from the hall and ran up, carrying his own rifle. The two boys covered the soldiers, who had backed into a group. Alana rounded from the wash-houses and advanced holding the Glock in her right hand, the left hand cupped under. She bent her knees and moved swiftly to cover the ground.

"Drop your weapons!" Stephen shouted, his voice boomed around the buildings, filling the space. One soldier threw his rifle straight to the ground. The rest, panicked, and with eyes searching, began to lay their weapons down.

Stephen called out, "Lieutenant Baxter. Come here!" His blood was running fast. He knew he didn't have much time before he ran out of adrenaline. No-one moved. "Lieutenant. Now!" He screamed the last word.

One of the soldiers pushed one of the men huddled amongst them. Others joined in and eventually Lieutenant Baxter staggered forward, jostled out of the group. Stephen saw he was young and frightened. Stephen holstered his Glock and beckoned him forward. Alana covered Baxter. When he came up, Stephen put a hand on Baxter's shoulder and unsheathed his hunting knife.

Retrieved from one of the dead soldiers, who had stolen it from Stephen, the knife was a 10 cm fixed blade of laminate steel on a grip shaped handle. Stephen rammed it into Baxter's neck. Blood spurted. The soldiers yelled and recoiled amongst themselves.

Alana called out, "Nobody move." Her authoritative voice restored order.

Stephen twisted the knife and withdrew the blade from Baxter's neck and let him fall to the ground. "Sergeant?!"

The soldiers began to panic, imagining themselves being picked off one by one in order of rank. Gary shot into the air then aimed back at the men. They were surrounded and, backed into a corner they could still be dangerous. The shot controlled them. "Sergeant?" Stephen sounded impatient. He was covered in Baxter's blood.

Movement at the end of the wash-houses. Alana turned round and bent her knees slightly. "Stop! Do not move."

From around the corner, the female Sergeant appeared and confidently approached. She had been at the toilets, Stephen realised, and suddenly appalled none of them had noticed. She carried her rifle across herself, with the muzzle pointed down. Her helmet was on and hooked in place. She ignored Alana pointing a gun at her and strode forward. A few paces away, she stopped, and said, "You called me?"

Stephen smiled at her.

27

ALL THE SOLDIERS had to take their boots, jackets, and shirts off. They were stripped of all weapons and herded into the church. Charlie and Vincent joined Phil in being an armed guard watching over them. Gareth was instructed that no-one was to touch the dead soldiers, but Stephen had removed Morgan's pistols. The Sergeant was allowed to keep her full uniform and rifle. They took her to the manse. After she'd fetched Karen from the vestry in the church, Alana made tea.

They sat round the kitchen table. Gary sat across from Stephen, who had washed his face of Lieutenant Baxter. The Sergeant stood with her back to the rear door. She eyed the canned food, which is what Stephen wanted her to see; that they had retaken their stolen belongings. Alana placed mugs on the table and poured the tea out a giant tea-pot. She caught Stephen's eye and he saw she was thinking the same thing as him. They had made love on the table during the night. He managed not to smirk.

Suspicious at first, the Sergeant waited until Stephen sipped at his tea. She lifted the mug up. "Any milk?"

"You killed most of our cows," said Stephen coldly.

The Sergeant blinked acknowledgement. She put down the mug and unhooked her helmet strap, took it off and placed it on the table across from Morgan's silver pistols, which lay with the grips facing her. She kept the rifle slung over her right shoulder but thought better of it and laid it up against the cans. Stephen introduced them all to her. He could tell she realised that if they had wanted her dead, she already would be. The Sergeant introduced herself as Lucy Pullman.

"Sit down, Sergeant Pullman," said Stephen. "Please."

Pullman sat down and sipped her tea. "I prefer coffee."

Stephen smiled. He glanced up at Alana, who was leaning against the worktop and watching Pullman intently.

He wanted to ask her now what she thought of the Sergeant, realising he valued her assessment and was beginning to rely on it. "Tell me about your unit."

"Ragtag group," said Pullman. "Some aren't even soldiers. We pick up strays as we go along."

Stephen thought of Phil and his two dead friends back at the farmhouse. "Are you a soldier?"

Pullman nodded. "Lancashire and Borders. Afghanistan, 2014. Back here when the virus took hold. Battle of Grangemouth." She sat back and shrugged. The oil refinery at Grangemouth had been destroyed in a battle for control in 2016. The part she was leaving out, Stephen realised, was five years of being a Sergeant in Morgan's Unit.

Stephen leaned forward. He looked at the silver pistols on the table, then straight at Pullman. "How would you like a promotion and some proper soldiering?"

"Depends." She returned Stephen's stare but she stayed sat back in her chair. "What have you got in mind?"

Stephen gestured around the room as if it were the whole village. "These are British citizens. Do your duty. Protect us. Don't leech off us."

Pullman thought about that. "How are you set up? Where's Rory?"

Stephen said, "Suzanne's in bed. Rory is our business. We're going to create a council; that's your government. We'll have judges; there's your judiciary. Gary's the General. Alana's Chief Constable. Karen runs the stables. And you'll be the Colonel."

Pullman looked at them in turn. Karen was smiling but everyone else was dead serious. The Sergeant asked Stephen, "And what do you do round here?"

Stephen sat back and said nothing. He stared at her and never moved.

Pullman closed her lips and Stephen saw her throat constrict as she swallowed. She took a sip of her tea. "And the men?"

"I'll help you get them into line, and you answer to Gary, but you run the unit the way you see fit. You train the rest of the villagers up as a militia."

"What do we eat?" Pullman was pushing now for concessions.

"Eat your fucking horses for all I care," said Stephen, knowing they clearly needed a base for winter, and that he held all the cards. He spoke more softly when he saw Karen frown. "Or go and catch more deer. Trade with the villagers for vegetables. They'll be glad of the venison."

Pullman sat up. She pulled her body armour. "OK," she said simply.

"Can you get the men in line?" Alana asked.

"Yes, ma'am," Sergeant Pullman said, sure of herself. She seemed tough to Stephen, having survived all this time as the only woman in a small army.

"Let me ask you some questions," said Stephen. Pullman nodded agreement. "The horses, guns, equipment. Who owns it? The unit or the individual soldier?"

Pullman's expression told Stephen she hadn't thought about. "British Army, I guess."

"Well here's your first order, Colonel," said Stephen. "The Chief Constable is taking possession of everyone's kit until we're sure they can be trusted. Except yours. You keep yours. Morgan, Weaver and Baxter; you and your men can bury them but their kit and horses belong to me."

Pullman nodded, though she looked a little unsure about the last part. Robbing dead soldiers would gall her, Stephen knew, but she agreed anyway. "Any more orders, sir?"

"Yeah," said Gary, asserting his new found position. "Get your men to sort our defences out. We've got a gate and a cattle-grid but it's just embarrassing when you ride around them."

"Yes, sir," Pullman said firmly. She stood up, careful not to startle them. She saluted. After a pause, Gary jumped to his feet and saluted her back.

Stephen didn't trust himself to give a convincing salute, so he pushed the silver pistols across the table. "Jump to it, Colonel."

28

STEPHEN LISTENED FROM the kitchen. He could
hear a young girl's voice. It was Karen, talking to Alana as
the younger girl got ready for bed. Despite not hearing any
actual words, it was good to hear Karen's voice for once
coming from the other room. Alana said something in reply
and then called out, "Stephen?"

He walked through to the front room. Karen was lying
on the couch, under the blankets while Alana kneeled to the
side, stroking the girl's hair. In the firelight, she looked
beautiful as she smiled at him. "Karen would like to give
you something."

Silently, and without looking at him, Karen held up a
soft sheet of paper. Found in a box under the sofa, along
with some crayons and pencils, the paper had a drawing on
it. After an encouraging look from Alana, Stephen took the
paper from Karen. He looked at it and his heart melted.
Karen had drawn herself and a horse. It was the drawing as
if done by a much younger child; green grass along the
bottom of the sheet and a strip of blue for the sky.
Unmistakable though was a man and woman to the left of
the horse; he and Alana. Underneath, in a childish scrawl
was written "thank you" copied from more grown up letters
above it.

"Thank you very much, Karen," he said. "You are very
welcome. May I keep this picture?"

Still not looking at him, Karen turned away and made
like she was sleeping. Alana spoke for her. "Yes, keep it.
Maybe put it on the fridge."

Before he left the room, he told Karen it was a very
good picture and went through to the kitchen. The manse
was otherwise empty with Phil and Gary pulling a night
duty guarding the soldiers, who had their boots and coats
returned to them. In the morning, the soldiers would begin
trenches around the village by day and patrol the perimeter

at night. All would be organised into shifts, in the belief that keeping the men busy kept them disciplined and out of trouble. Stephen had already put the fear of God into them and a first night in a draughty church would help.

A small wood fire burned in a pot perched on the electric stove. Using it for light, he found the fridge where a couple of magnets held old notes. Stephen rearranged the magnets, stuck the drawing up, and thought of another picture which had once been made for him; Jack's painting of his Mum and Dad. Stephen had placed that other picture on another fridge using different magnets.

Alana came in. He had made tea and she poured herself a mug and slumped down on the chair. "Not many of these tea bags left," she said.

"Enjoy them while they last." Stephen leaned back as he tried to square the picture on the fridge. "I think you're taller than me in this picture."

She chuckled softly and sipped at the tea. He sat down across from and asked, "What do you make of our new Colonel?"

"I think she'll be fine. Lucy Pullman will rise to the rank."

Stephen sighed and looked at the roof. "Three more deaths today," he said finally.

She looked at him straight on. Her tone was cold, like a clear mountain loch, but not without compassion. "Why not kill them all?"

He shrugged and blew out a sigh. He could feel regret building behind his eyes. "Same as Phil, I guess."

"Yes, same as Phil," she said, her tone soft but insistent that he should listen and not just hear. "That night you found us. He was one of the two who brought us up the road. I could tell he was scared and didn't want to be there. But he would have hurt us, Stephen. He would have done what his friends wanted him to do."

He felt his neck bend and his head flopped over. She

went on, "And those soldiers would have done the same thing. Can you imagine what winter would have been like with them here and Morgan in charge? And Rory? Me and Karen would not have waited to find out."

Stephen breathed. "Morgan would have kept them in line."

"I doubt it," she said quickly. "I've locked all their gear in the police cell. But there isn't much of it. Sure, they've had access to a large cache of weapons and ammunition in the past, but there's not much left."

"Really?" He was shocked.

"And how tough was Morgan, really? How did we really take him out? Because of our superior training and firepower? No, because he'd gotten soft and when his men ran out of ammo they would have run out of discipline and this whole place would have gone up in smoke."

He knew she was right. "Can Pullman keep discipline?"

"Maybe." Alana sipped her tea again. "You know she could have taken us out don't you?"

"I've been thinking about that," agreed Stephen. "How did she slip away? To the toilets for crying out loud. And then she just walked round the corner."

"So why didn't she just shoot you?" Alana asked but he guessed she knew the answer.

"She wanted the Colonel out the way?"

"Maybe, but maybe she just wanted to be a soldier again. Even if you were going to kill her, she wanted to go out with her boots on."

Stephen thought about that and tried to understand the implication. "So, we keep on her good side."

"No. You," said Alana, pointedly, "you keep her in line."

29

MORNING ARRIVED WITH Phil and Gary entering the house, after guarding the soldiers all night. Cold and tired, they slumped down in the kitchen. Stephen came in after them and asked them how they were.

Gary yawned. "We're fine. We've left Charlie looking after them. But two of them cleared off in the night."

"Two of the soldiers?"

"Yeah," said Phil. "I took them outside for a piss and they just legged it."

Stephen paused. "What did you do?"

Phil looked at Gary. They both looked worried. Gary said, "We just let them go. No point shooting them. They never took anything with them."

"And they just ran towards the trees," Phil added.

"Okay," said Stephen. "Right decision." The two boys grinned at each other as Stephen started to fix some breakfast.

Stephen went out to inspect the troops. The soldiers were lined up and standing to attention. Newly promoted Colonel Pullman walked alongside, her rifle stowed somewhere in the church. Behind them, in the manse's large garden, Alana was running a horse in a circle while Karen bobbed happily on its back. The men glanced warily at each other out the corner of their eyes but they did their best to concentrate on standing to attention. Gary and Phil fell in behind Stephen and Pullman. Charlie and Vincent had been let go but they hung back at the burnt-out hall, observing.

Stephen stood and faced them. There were five now. Weak sunshine, diffused by a thin high cloud, warmed their shoulders. They looked tough and weathered. At least they could consolidate the ammunition, thought Stephen. He waited a moment before speaking.

"Good morning, men. My name is Stephen Arnott. Last night, Davis and Anderson deserted. Today, you have the same choice. Leave now, with the clothes on your back. Like they did."

Stephen waited. Eyes swivelled amongst the ranks, looking at what the others might do. He went on, "Or stay. You will work, you will train, and you will do your duty. Eventually, you will have your weapons back. You can hunt for food and you can defend this village."

He waited again. Turning to Pullman, he asked, "Do these men agree, Colonel Pullman?"

In full Sergeant mode, Pullman yelled out, "You heard the man. Do you agree?"

"Yes, sir!" they shouted in unison.

Stephen nodded to Pullman. She called out the order to stand at ease and the men complied. Leaving Gary and Phil where they were, Stephen went to the head of the line. Pullman walked with him. At the first man, Stephen asked firmly, "Name?"

The soldier swallowed. "Talbot, sir."

"Where you from, Talbot?"

"Wolverhampton, sir."

Stephen smiled at the corner of his mouth. "How's the Wanderers doing this season?"

Without missing a beat, Talbot answered Stephen's question about a football team who, of course, hadn't existed for years, "Terrible, sir. Haven't won a game."

Some of the men sniggered and one openly laughed. Pullman shouted, "Hold your line!" They straightened their backs and stopped laughing. However, their reactions to both the joke and Pullman pleased Stephen. It showed him they had some morale and the potential for discipline.

"You up for defending this village, Talbot?" Stephen asked.

Talbot twisted narrow eyes to look at Stephen. "Hell yes, sir." He had spoken quietly and convincingly. He held the look for a moment before focusing his eyes back forward.

Stephen moved across the line and had similar discussions with Moore, Gibson, O'Neill, and Mills. He went back to facing them. "Your first order is feeding the horses. Your second order is to set up some defences for the village."

Stephen looked to Pullman. She nodded and ordered Talbot to lead the men to the lower part of the village where they would find what they needed. Ironically, Stephen had told her, there was plenty of feed now there were only a few cows left. The men were dismissed and double-timed it down the road past the cattle-grid. Stephen nodded to Gary and Phil who fell back quietly to go the other way and observe what the soldiers actually did.

Left alone with Pullman, Stephen asked her, "You up for this task, Colonel?" He was wondering if she had any lingering animosity over her commanders being killed.

She grinned. "Hell yes, sir." Her eyes crinkled up and she seemed genuinely happy.

Reassured, he asked her, "Any thoughts about ditches?"

She nodded eagerly. She beckoned him to move with her to the grassy pathway which led out the village. The gate of twisted scrap metal stood quietly. Pointing up the road a bit, she said, "I think we should dig a trench from there and bring it to the bend in the road."

Stephen followed her gesture as it arced out, passing Gareth's gate, until it met the road further down. "A big ditch."

"It's the right thing to do. Any horses running at it would be greatly impeded."

"And our horses?" He emphasised how the horses belonged to them all and not just the soldiers.

"I've thought about that," Pullman said. She stepped back a bit to demonstrate better. She held up her hands in front of Gareth's scrap-yard gate. "We take this apart and rebuild it as a proper gate. Make it easy for our horses to get out and harder for others to get in."

Stephen nodded agreement. "What about your men?"

Pullman rearranged her feet until she was square on him. "I'll keep them in line. I'll need a Sergeant and implement a night patrol."

Stephen could see what she was thinking. "Engineering through the day and discipline through the night."

"Indeed, sir," said Pullman.

"Your Sergeant?"

"Probably Talbot," she said, "But I'll make them all seek it on merit."

"Competition?" said Stephen.

"Commitment and loyalty," she corrected.

Stephen nodded again and appraised this capable woman. He held out a hand. Surprised at first, she took it and they shook agreement. He said, gesturing at the proposed trench, "We'll involve the whole village in this." Over at the hall, Charlie nudged Vincent and they headed back down the high street.

30

STEPHEN CALLED EVERYONE together. Gary and Phil came in from a day on the ditches. Alana and Karen had been tending the horses. They waited on Stephen to speak. He had spent the day with Charlie, having walked round the village, from the ditch works to the distillery. Inspecting the warehouses, which remained locked and secure, they talked about the set-up of the council. A few days previously, the villagers had decided on a council of four people, with two judges. Soldiers wouldn't be able to vote.

"It's time to plan out what we're doing next," he said finally.

Gary frowned. "What do you mean? It's all under control."

"We're about to elect a council," explained Stephen. Gary shrugged; he knew this. "And once they get a grip of decisions they'll want to take control of things."

"So, we don't let them," said Gary. When he didn't get a sympathetic response, he looked to Alana. She remained quiet, having already discussed this with Stephen. Karen sat quietly, watching the exchange intently. Gary slumped back in his seat.

Stephen leaned forward. He spoke quietly. "We need an exit strategy. If things turn against us, we need to be sure what we are going to do."

"Things won't turn against us," said Gary. "Look at what we've done for everyone."

"People are already complaining about having to dig the trench," said Alana.

"That's true," said Phil. "I've heard it."

"That won't go on forever. The ditch will only take so long." Gary was dismissive.

Stephen put a hand on his arm. "Watch what happens after the vote tonight. You'll see."

Gary was caught by the thought. He relaxed. "Okay. What do we do? I mean, you're asking, but you two have already decided." He moved his gaze between Stephen and Alana, who glanced at each other. Phil looked at his hands on the table. Karen stood beside Alana.

Stephen said, "After the vote, you and Phil go to the bunker. Make sure it's secure. Leave in the dark. Come back in the dark."

Gary looked again from Stephen to Alana. There was hostility in his eyes. "What will you do?"

"We'll carry on like nothing is the matter," Alana answered evenly. "We'll be here when you get back."

"Now why would you say that?" Gary said, raising his voice. "I never even thought that."

"Settle down, Gary." Phil tried to reason with him. He placed a hand on Gary's shoulder.

"Get off," Gary shouted and stood up. His chair scraped along the floor. He stormed out. Phil went after him.

31

VOTES WERE CAST in the church. Using the old collection box, which had a slot for visitors' money, each person cast their vote. From the ten people who stood, Charlie and Frank joined two others, Jean and Linda, on the Council. Bet and Wilma became judges; two fierce women no-one would mess with. Suzanne had not stood for any office, the rumour being she was upset at not just having her authority simply handed back.

Warm firelight lit the room. With everyone gathered inside, spread out amongst the pews, it felt safe and normal. Charlie got up to speak, "Thank you everyone. As agreed, we'll vote again next year. The Council will run the village on behalf of the people. The Judges will arbitrate on disagreements, by the authority of the Council, but independent of it."

Frank asked, trying to be jovial, "A speech already, Charlie?"

There was a big laugh. Smiling, Charlie said, "You're right. Let's toast the future. Slàinte." He raised a glass of whisky. There were choruses of agreement and everyone drank. After that, there was applause.

Charlie stayed on his feet. "And for all of this, we must thank a few people." He looked around before raising a glass towards Stephen. "To our friends; Mr Arnott and his family. Thank you."

Another sip of the whisky and some more applause. Alana leaned into Stephen during the noise and said, "Family?" Stephen laughed. He looked across the room at Gary leaning against the wall, still in the huff. Phil stood quietly next to him.

Charlie was still on his feet. Expectant faces listened. "We have done so much in the last few weeks. It's hard work on the defences, but worth it. Our army leads us in this endeavour."

Applause and another dram. Stephen and Alana looked at each other, noting the phrase "our army". Karen stood, watching everything.

"There is one thing we must decide though," said Charlie. He made a show of looking round the room but his attention was on Stephen. "We have a council and judges but we need a police force."

A few people looked down, unsure of bringing this up. Gary straightened up and looked over at Stephen, seeing now what Stephen had meant earlier. Phil, surprisingly, spoke up. "When Paul was your Constable, did he take care of Rory?"

Some mumbles of agreement. Charlie spoke loudly, "And what did happen to Rory?" Hush spread across the room. Rory's fate, and that of his friends, had been unspoken aloud until now. Seeing Stephen's expression, as he glared at him across the church, Charlie softened. "We are grateful to be free of him. But we also need access to the weapons."

Having considered these topics might be aired, Stephen and Alana stayed motionless and impassive. A general hubbub of discussions arose as they waited for someone else to speak. Frank, for his part, just looked at his feet.

Stephen stood. Charlie made a show of conceding the floor. Stephen waited for a moment before speaking. "The weapons belong to the British Army. They will be issued to its soldiers when the time is right. As for the police, I have already decided that Alana is the Chief Constable for this area."

No-one moved. The church was silent. Charlie stared at Stephen, unsettling him with calm focus, seemingly having prepared his own responses and facial expressions. However, Stephen stood his ground, letting them all wonder if Charlie would challenge him further. Gary was right, thought Stephen, the people knew he had freed them from Rory and Morgan, but he also knew things were turning. Feeling secure, as Alana had put it, was making the villagers look in a different direction. Charlie was attempting to seize the situation. Not so long ago, he was ready to leave with Vincent when Morgan had stated his intent to stay.

As Alana stood up beside him, Stephen imagined some of those thoughts transmitted to the look he gave Charlie. They walked to the door and met up with Gary and Phil who caught up at the door. Stephen looked back into the room. "Make no mistake. Have your council and your judges. But remember who gave you them."

He and his "family" left. Almost immediately, loud voices could be heard inside. Outside, Gary said, "You were right. Those bastards."

"Don't worry about that now," said Stephen. He put his hands on the boy's shoulders. "You've got your mission."

Gary nodded and smiled gratefully. He thumped Phil on the shoulder. They ran off into the night, unseen. Stephen and Alana made their way quickly to the kitchen in manse. Whilst Karen slept in the other room, they checked their weapons, locked the outside doors and kept watch all night.

32

STEPHEN NODDED AWAKE at first light. He could have kicked himself. How long had he slept? He looked across the hall and saw Alana at the other window, her head on the ledge, sound asleep. He looked out his own window. The village was quiet.

A band of yellow on the horizon was lifting the gloom of the sky. The meeting in the church had gone on for a while but had broken up quietly. A few drunken laughs were heard, not the storming of the manse he and Alana had feared. Once Gary and Phil got back with news of the bunker's condition, they could make an informed decision about their next move.

Gareth and Bet went out to their positions on the gate without glancing up at the manse. Beyond that, Stephen could make out the line of the trench works, spades and shovels lying at rest. Staked out, it would lead from just past the gate round to the bend in the road which led to the lower part of the distillery. At that point, a cliff and the sea would keep anyone else away.

Now on top of his gate, something caught Gareth's eye. Stephen shifted his position to see what it was. His movement disturbed Alana. She shook herself awake. Outside, Gareth jumped down and ran as best he could up the grassy path, which led away from the village to the forest. Coming towards him were two people. One of them had an arm over the other's shoulder, dragging him along due to injuries. Moments later, Bet was banging at the manse door, shouting, "Stephen! We need you, Stephen!"

33

WITH PHIL AND Gary away, Stephen was loathe to leave
Alana behind with Karen but she urged him to go. "We'll
be fine, here," she had said and patted her SA80. It had
been Weaver's and, despite its worn condition, worked well.
He kissed her goodbye.

When he stepped out the house, he waved in at them
through the window. Astonished, he heard Karen's voice
through the glass. "Where is Stephen going?" Alana
answered her but Stephen couldn't hear the reply clearly.
He walked down the path and met Colonel Pullman and
Private Talbot. They were already mounted on their horses.
Private Moore held the reins of Stephen's horse, Sabre,
which had formerly belonged to Morgan.

He saw Pullman watch him closely as he put his left foot
in the stirrup. He bounced his right foot and pulled himself
up. When he had settled in the saddle, Moore stepped back.
Pullman smiled at him. "Been on a horse much?"

"A couple of times," Stephen said, referring to pony
trekking on holidays past, though he knew he was busted.
Talbot grinned at him as the soldier nudged his feet on the
sides of his horse and moved off.

Stephen did the same thing and Sabre trotted after.
Pullman, mounted on Bess, followed and they caught up
with Talbot. They rounded the cattle grid and headed up
the grassy path.

"No Gary and Phil?" Pullman asked.

"Nah," said Stephen. "I've got them doing something
else." He saw Pullman and Talbot exchange a look making
Stephen feel suddenly vulnerable. Until recently, he had
spent a lot of time on his own, and was now beginning to
realise he was relying on others a lot. Being on his own with
two soldiers, Gary and Phil out in the hills, and Alana and
Karen back at the village, he also felt overstretched.

Even this trip, to investigate why Scott and Rob had

been attacked in the woods, Stephen found himself with two others, people he barely knew, relying on their insight and training. He would have travelled alone until recently and would even have left this trip to others. Still, he thought, you can't set yourself up as the law and then not uphold it. It had all started with Gary, of course, befriending him and teaming up. He struggled to remember how that had even happened.

As they rode up the hill, leaving the village quietly behind, he began to fret over Alana, and strange little, mostly silent, Karen. A small girl, who spoke to Alana like a chatterbox, and not to anyone else, gave him a purpose other than the dread over Ellen and Jack. He was not really worried, though. Alana could take care of them both and no-one else even knew the boys were out the village. He would go up here, have a word with Joseph, or whoever was up there, and be back before dark.

The path became a little more pronounced, having been cut when it was being used as an access road to the forestry land. Horses' hooves clopped on stones as they kept going. Pullman asked, "You've met this Joseph?"

"Yep," said Stephen. "He was a bit different from the others I've met. The woods have had people in them for a while."

"What's up there, though?" asked Talbot.

"Just trees," said Stephen. "When you brought back deer I was surprised. I thought the biggest animals up there were squirrels."

Pullman and Talbot exchanged another look. There was definitely something on their minds, and Stephen wondered if there was something else going on between them. Pullman looked back at Stephen like she was going to say something, but she stopped herself.

Stephen pulled the reins back and Sabre came to a halt. "What is it?" The other two pulled up, their backs to him.

Expertly, Pullman backed her horse up to be level with

Stephen. Just as skillfully, Talbot turned his around to face them both. She said eventually, "We took a kicking up there for those deer."

That surprised Stephen and then he thought of their exhaustion on returning to the village the day he had killed the officers. "What happened?"

Talbot looked off to the side, embarrassed by the tale as Pullman told it. "Morgan shot the first deer, but he only clipped it. Talbot and the Lieutenant went after it. Next thing you know, they come riding back out chased by a gang of crazies."

"They were waiting for us," said Talbot in mitigation. "And we'd stumbled on their camp. All armed with rocks and crappy spears."

Pullman picked up the story, "So Morgan orders us to engage. We drop a few but there are dozens."

"Dozens?" Stephen checked. As far as anyone had thought, there were only a few nomads picking on the berries and easting roast mice for tea.

"Dozens," said Talbot. "Eventually we scared them off but Gibson and O'Neill took a brick to the head each."

Pullman added, "We got our deer and bugged out. By chance, Weaver got another one on the way back."

"Shit." Stephen sighed. "Is this what we're walking into?"

"Sorry, sir," said Pullman. "We should have said."

Stephen nodded in stern agreement but then he changed tack. "What options do we have?"

A breeze brushed the grass. They were near the reservoir and it reflected the grey sky. Water trickled through the dam overflow and headed to the Margaretvale river mouth. Talbot spoke first. "I've an idea."

34

STEPHEN AND THE Colonel approached the camp on foot, leading their horses. Grimy faces watched their every move. Dozens of people, spread over a good-sized area, were living in the woods. They dressed in old and patched clothing, some with two thin jackets and others with soot-blackened puffed coats.

Children played and ran around but the adults just stared. Camp fires crackled in front of lean-to shelters of reclaimed materials and wood. They had been allowed through a narrow path, leading from the old access road. Logs had been formed into a gate and pulled back to allow them through.

Making their way through the camp, they saw pens with pigs in them, and a few chickens behind a high fence. A woman inside the fence held up an egg and stared coldly at Stephen and Pullman.

Pitched at the end of the path was a large tent. It looked like it had once been a marquee tent, the sort of thing you would see at a garden party, but it had been modified. Forming a circle, and domed at the top, it now resembled a yurt, like it belonged to a Mongolian ruler. Tent flaps were formed by two large tartan blankets, out of place in this setting. One was pulled aside and out stepped Joseph, easily recognisable from Stephen's last encounter, his face was open and smiling.

"Greetings," he said as his visitors stopped. He was dressed in clean clothes, made from wool and made into fine blue cloth. His feet were in some kind of hide boots.

Stephen looked around. Nothing seemed threatening. "Greetings, Joseph. My name is Stephen."

"I know who you are, Stephen." Joseph pointed across to a clearing where Privates Davis and Anderson sat by a fire. They did not meet Pullman's eyes. Joseph said, "Your woman pulled a gun on me. You have brought a soldier this time."

Ignoring this, Stephen said, "You assaulted two of our people."

"They were attempting to take our wood," Joseph said evenly as if this explained everything.

"These woods belong to the Crown," said Stephen.

Joseph's face fell into a cold glare. He walked up to Stephen. "Crown? Whose crown?"

Stephen said, "And this soldier represents the British Army."

Joseph looked Pullman up and down. "British Army. There is no Britain, Stephen. There is your village and our forest." One of Joseph's men ran up through the woods. Joseph held up a hand to Stephen and Pullman, indicating they should wait. Pullman tensed slightly at the movement but did nothing. The runner stopped, nodded to Joseph, who nodded back and gestured as if for him to come forward. Instead, the man turned and ran away.

"It doesn't have to be like this, Joseph," said Stephen. "We can trade. We've got whisky. We could trade you for wood. You would come under the protection of the British Army."

Joseph smiled indulgently. "Whisky. Trade." He chuckled, passing time while waiting on something. Stephen felt the situation slipping away from him though he had expected this would not have been the same as when he had scared Joseph off before. After hearing Pullman's story of Morgan's Unit being overwhelmed, Stephen had imagined the people in the forest were becoming more organised, perhaps bolder, but he had not imagined this. Joseph had created a society, Stephen saw, probably through sheer personality, but it functioned all the same.

Twigs snapped to their left. The man came back, this time with Talbot by the scruff of his neck. Another man led Talbot's horse and carried his rifle. Talbot was thrown to the ground beside Pullman. She knelt quickly to help him.

His hands were tied and blood ran down his head, having been captured while he tried to wheel around and approach from the rear; his plan to outflank Joseph's group.

Stephen kept his attention on Joseph. He wore that same knowing smile he had the day they first met. Stephen reached for his Glock, which was under his coat. Joseph reached out a hand to still him. "This is our forest. You may leave."

Pullman had freed Talbot and helped him to his feet. The man with the horse handed the reins to Talbot and the rifle to Joseph. Stephen backed up, his hand on the pistol grip. Joseph lifted the weapon in both hands and stretched out his arms, handing it to Talbot.

"Take it," said Joseph, as if to a child. "Take it and go."

Talbot looked to the side, anticipating a trick, but seeing none, he took the rifle from Joseph. Pullman had her hand to a knife and was stepping back. Stephen began to relax. Joseph used a benevolent smile as he said, "It was a pleasure to see you. Go and be safe. But never return."

"I thought you would have kept the rifle," said Stephen.

"There is no need," said Joseph, airily. Then his eyes narrowed as he said, "We have other weapons."

Stephen looked around. Blank faces stared at them. They showed no emotion which made Stephen very nervous in their stillness. He caught Pullman's attention and the three of them backed off. Bodies pressed against them, alarming the horses. They kept going. When they reached the wooden gate, they hastily mounted their horses. Soot-smeared faces drifted back amongst the trees.

35

THE RAIN HAD stayed off. "We won't get trench-foot, lad," remarked Frank. Everyone laughed as Stephen shovelled a load up and out the trench along with the others. Phil was further up, clearing gorse with the soldiers, while Gary worked alongside Stephen and Frank.

The trench was coming on. At a meter deep and two meters wide, they had made it half-way to their objective. There was continuing discontent amongst some of the village about being pressed into service. Even Stephen was beginning to wonder why they had started it as his back felt the strain of another shovel load.

September sunshine had faded to October skies and nothing further had been heard from the forest. Only the soldiers ventured up there to hunt for deer and were returning unharmed. But the silence troubled Stephen; what were the forest folk up to? On his and Phil's return, Gary had reported their bunker was still intact. They could leave here, and go there any time, but Stephen felt compelled to stay. He knew he was not being honest with himself, or others, for his reasons, but stay he did and the others stayed with him.

He threw his shovel into the dirt and leaned his foot on it. He pressed the handle down and lifted another shovel load out.

He looked to Gary to see what he was doing but he was standing still. "Having a rest, Gary?" Stephen shouted out. Gary's jaw was open. Frank was looking up the road and Stephen noticed everyone on the line rest their shovels and look up.

Gary said, "Listen."

Stephen lifted his head and stilled his breathing. He could hear a low buzzing. It rose in tone then paused and resumed at a lower tone. It grew louder. The tone changed again. It was an engine, changing gears. They all started to recognise it, a petrol engine. Stephen shouted, "Colonel!"

Pullman and Talbot left the soldiers further up the trench and ran up the road. She threw the Private her rifle and she drew her Browning pistol. They ran up the road and knelt down either side of the tarmac. Talbot pressed the SA80 into his shoulder and eyed the sight. Pullman sighted her pistol up the road and waited. Stephen slapped Gary on the arm to go and fetch his rifle. The boy gathered his and wits ran off to the manse.

The vehicle was coming closer. They could hear the engine getting louder. Finally, round the bend they saw a white SUV trundle round. As it came closer, Stephen could see it had black letters painted on the side: UN. The SUV slowed down as it approached and stopped about 200 metres from where Talbot and Pullman were. It had turned at an angle.

It sat there for a few moments, its engine idling. To Stephen's left, he saw Gary run out the manse and take up a position parallel to Pullman. He leaned into his rifle and eyed up the sights, aiming at the truck. Finally, the rear passenger door behind the driver opened and someone stepped out.

He was tall and wearing a blue helmet, its paint all chipped, and a Kevlar vest which covered his body. Large yellow letters on the vest and helmet proclaimed: PRESS. He took short steps in his cargo trousers and boots. Empty hands were outstretched. "Good afternoon," he called out in a southern English accent, his eyes moving from the diggers to the soldiers and back again. "Is there someone in charge I may speak to?"

Everyone looked at Stephen, who was looking into the truck. Someone else was in the back while two people sat up front. The driver kept his hands on the steering wheel, while the other clearly had a pump-action shotgun in his lap, pointing at the roof. The person in the back was moving around, trying to see out.

Stephen pulled himself out the trench. "You can talk to me."

"May I come forward?" the man called out.

Stephen beckoned him to approach. Gary followed him with the rifle, while the soldiers covered the truck. As he came closer, Stephen was shocked to see that he recognised this man. He was a television journalist from before the virus; Thomas Townsend. He was smiling and he kept his empty hands held away from his side.

"Good afternoon, sir," said Townsend.

"Good afternoon," replied Stephen, cordially. "Are you from the UN?"

Townsend frowned briefly. "No. We just use one of their old trucks. We're from the American Broadcast News Service."

Stephen almost gasped. "I heard a report the Americans were hit as bad as us."

"They were," said Townsend. He seemed to be weighing Stephen up, eyeing the surroundings; their village, trenches, and soldiers. "But things are beginning to change."

Stephen looked around. He jutted a chin at the truck. "Who have you brought?"

Townsend glanced over his shoulder. "Camera operator; driver." He paused before adding, "Guard."

"Are you looking for trouble, Mr Townsend?" said Stephen, revealing he knew the man's name.

"No," smiled Townsend, grateful for being recognised. "We're here for the news."

"Well," said Stephen. "You better come tell us some."

36

TOWNSEND SET UP in the church. The driver parked the SUV out front and the guard stayed at the truck, after persuasion by the journalist, because Stephen would not allow him inside with his shotgun. From the back-seat emerged the other passenger, a female camera operator introduced as "Just Sue." She hoisted an old beat-up looking camera onto her shoulder and lit a powerful light on a stand she had set up earlier. Townsend held a microphone wrapped in fur on the end of a pole and placed headphones on his head.

As everyone gathered in the pews, he spoke, looking into the camera. The hubbub around him masked what he was saying. Stephen and his "family" took their customary place and Karen sat down in between them and rested her head on Alana's arm. They ignored Charlie and his growing entourage who sat further down.

Townsend turned to the congregation and called out, "Thank you for coming. Please, take a seat." The last of the villagers took their seats. Vincent, still dirty from digging, sat next to Charlie. "Thanks again. Your welcome is gratefully received." Townsend raised a glass of whisky he had been given earlier.

"Is the telly back on, then?" someone shouted. Alana smiled at Stephen. He found himself laughing along with everyone else.

Once the laughter had died down, Townsend said seriously, "In America, yes. Here? I don't believe so." He went on to tell them about how he came to be here filming.

Like many others in the south-east of Britain, he had fled across the water from the virus. Things were bad there, too, like everywhere. French authorities were unable to help much but Americans had come to the refugee camps and did the best they could. Journalists filming for the ABNS, the American Broadcast News Service, had recognised

Townsend. He had been offered a job touring around Britain to file news reports about the situation.

What he found echoed the news brought by Malcolm in the yacht "The Mercury". There were isolated pockets of places similar to their village, some terrible lawless places, but mostly what they found was empty land. Official estimates put the population of the former UK at under two million.

There were gasps from the congregation when they heard that. Charlie called out, "That would make sixty million dead?"

"At least," said Townsend. "The virus got the most; the civil war got many; famine and other disease; murder."

He listed the causes of death like some far away statistic, thought Stephen, and he felt a few eyes on him. Something Townsend had said popped back into Stephen's head. "You said 'former' UK?"

"Indeed I did," said Townsend. "There is no UK Government anymore, let alone Scotland or Wales. We're not sure about Ireland but we do know about Orkney and Shetland."

Townsend was letting the people take in the information bit by bit, pausing after each new item. It explained his confusion about his query on the UN, thought Stephen, Townsend had not realised the news never reached here. There was probably no UN either. There were a few whispers and murmuring in the room but mostly people kept quiet and listened. Some asked about Orkney and Shetland.

"Claimed back by Norway," said Townsend, "though there are American troops on the ground in Shetland."

"What for?" Pullman had stood up.

Townsend looked around the room. "They are guarding Sullom Voe oil terminal. Production is up and running in the North Sea too in a joint effort between the US and Norway."

"Are the troops coming here?" Pullman sounded angry all of a sudden. The mood in the room was changing. Sue swivelled the camera around catching the reactions.

Stephen saw that Alana noticed this. She leaned into him. "He's here to find the news, not tell it." He nodded in understanding and thought about Malcolm telling him he had seen some mysterious activity on the north-east horizon; those ships were probably involved in oil production.

Townsend managed to calm everyone down by talking over them. "We don't know what their plans are but my sense is that no, they won't come here."

There was hush. Everyone was thinking, why not? If the Americans had enough of a society to dig for oil, send troops, and finance journalists, then why were they not doing more? Townsend took a sip of his whisky. His hand was shaking. He said, "Your whisky is very good. And what a lovely church. What happened to your hall?"

Heads turned to Stephen. He calmly looked back at Townsend and said nothing despite the camera pointing at him. Changing the subject, Townsend told them the rest.

The south-east remained the least populated. People had fled north when they couldn't get on the boats across the channel. There was talk of rebuilding a civilian government backed by France and Germany, but no-one Townsend had spoken to knew where the Royals were. When he spoke about that, Stephen glanced at Pullman. She had told him how she had shot refugees trying to get on board the HMS Defender, as it left Rosyth, with the royal family on board. Having fled from Balmoral, they had boarded in Fife and headed off, leaving Pullman as a Sergeant in Colonel Morgan's unit.

Townsend explained how Europe was just as badly hit by the virus but were getting organised again. The larger landmass meant more people were around. In the British Isles, defences like the M74 wall and the Manchester bombings had failed to contain the spread of the virus. When he had finished, there were few people with an appetite for more news.

37

STEPHEN SAT AT the end of the pier. He let his feet dangle off the edge. The horizon was blank. Frank sat further on at the end of the moorings and dozed while his fishing rod did the work. On the shore, Karen and Alana walked along, picking up stones and throwing them in the water. Waves gulped against the pier and washed the pebble beach.

When he heard footsteps, Stephen turned around. Townsend was walking towards him, alone. "May I join you?" he asked and gestured to a spot next to Stephen. When Stephen nodded, Townsend eased himself down. He was stiff, and he looked older than when he had been on television. He breathed in the clear air.

They sat in silence for a few minutes. Frank was beginning to snore which made Stephen laugh lightly. Townsend joined in. "Lovely day, isn't it?"

Stephen felt sorry for the journalist, trying to break the ice. He looked at him seriously. "Why won't the Americans come and help us?"

Townsend breathed in, realising the ice had broken. "They're almost in as bad shape as us. What resources they can spare are allocated to rebuilding some sort of infrastructure."

Stephen thought about that. "And our oil is helping them."

"East Lothian is beautiful, Stephen. But there's nothing here worth having." Townsend was speaking plainly, perhaps feeling he was expected to, but he softened it by adding, "In the grand scheme of things. Except your whisky."

Stephen couldn't help himself but smile. "Why wasn't it as bad over there?"

"It was as bad, apparently. Why we're in this state, I don't know. But there's something about the virus people don't know."

Stephen shrugged. "What's there to know now? We're all immune."

"That's the thing," said Townsend. He looked around as if they would be overheard. "Some might have had a low dose of it; sick then recovered. But the thing about the virus is, most of us left just never caught it."

Stephen blew air out. He had to let that thought sink in. The implication was staggering. It was blind luck they were still there. They sat and listened to the water for a while. Stephen finally asked, "So why are you here?"

"Don't underestimate the US affection for England, Stephen."

"England?" He smiled at the endearing trait of Americans to refer to Britain as England.

Townsend started to get animated. He kept his voice low so as not to wake Frank, but he spoke with urgency. "But it's my job to go beyond that. At the moment, American viewers see a far-off land where a war rages. Soon, they will see places like yours and see the real people. Then, they'll want to do something."

Stephen nodded. He could understand that. "So what do you want to do here?"

Townsend spoke even quieter. There was a slight tremor in his voice, as if scared. "I'd like to be able to talk to people and ask them about their experiences."

Stephen shrugged. He had no intention of standing in Townsend's way. He could do what he liked.

Townsend leaned in, "The good things. And the bad."

Stephen nodded. Now he understood. The journalist had already been talking to people in the village and he was probably starting to hear stories of recent developments. He guessed they were from Charlie, directly or not. Then Townsend added, "We would want to hear all sides."

Stephen looked coldly. "Are you looking for confessions?"

"No, no, no, no."

"I'm not finished." Stephen held up a hand. Alana and Karen had left the beach and were walking down the pier. When they heard Stephen's tone they stopped. Townsend blinked and swallowed. Stephen went on, "Cross the river. Walk up the shore, there's narrow track just up from the beach. There's a gorse bush, huge, which masks a short hollow. Are you following this?"

Townsend nodded, his face pale.

"In that hollow, there are three bodies. They'll be a state now but people from here will recognise them. We're free now, because those three bodies are there."

"Are you threatening me?"

Stephen huffed a laugh. "Are you recording me?"

"No," said Townsend. "I swear I'm not."

"Well, maybe you should have," said Stephen. Frank shuddered awake at the raised voices. "You could listen again to what I said." Alana and Karen made the final few steps and sat next to Stephen.

Townsend said, "I meant no offence, Mr-"

Stephen pointed out beyond the river. "If you're looking for an atrocity, you'll find it up there. If you want to know what happened here, dig up the church yard. If you think the choices I've made have been easy, then report it." He breathed heavily out his nose and then said more quietly. "Help us. Or, take your car and clear off."

Townsend waited for a moment. He looked like he was about to say something, before he thought better of it, and puffed to his feet and left. Alana placed her head on Stephen's shoulder. Frank went back to sleep.

38

THE SUV STARTED its engine. Stephen heard it trundle over the cattle grid. From his place in front of the fire, he listened to the engine recede into the distance. Suzanne glanced out her window as the vehicle climbed the hill and left.

Popping from the wood fire replaced the car sounds. Suzanne turned back to Stephen. She smiled and poured him some of her nettle tea. Using a fine tea set with burgundy roses for pattern, Stephen lifted the small cup and sipped. It was bitter but he smiled graciously. "Thanks for seeing me, Suzanne."

"It is nice of you to visit." She had lost weight and seemed nervous where once she had been imperious. "But I'm curious as to why you are here."

"And I'm curious as to where you have been." He looked around at her well kept front room. He sat on a comfortable sofa, facing her matching chair, on a worn carpet. Once-white cloth fitted the arm rests. A mechanical clock clicked on the mantelpiece.

"I've been keeping out of your way," she said, looking him in the eye.

"You are not an obstacle," he said, surprised at her response.

She laughed. "Oh, I would have been."

He did not know how to respond to that. He thought of the things he had had to do; Morgan, Rory. She looked at him, as if by reading his face, she could read his mind.

"You have done what no-one else could do," she began. "Or would do. We live in gratitude. And fear."

"Fear?" He couldn't believe it.

She ignored his protestation and continued her point. "And by defeating the enemies of this village, by freeing us, you have emboldened us."

Stephen stared into the fire. Yellow flames danced

around the wooden logs. "What's your point?"

She perched on the end of her chair. "Relinquish control. Take up the role of policeman. But let the council do its business. And stop the digging. There's no-one left to attack us."

"Oh, yes there is," said Stephen, thinking of what Joseph who had told him. *We have other weapons.*

Suzanne clapped her hands together and rubbed her palms. "I'm sorry you didn't find Ellen here. She was a lovely girl."

Stephen's eyes felt heavy. Her words resurrected his guilt at clinging to Alana in the night. He wondered if Jack would have been as good with a rifle as Gary and if he would even want that for his own son.

"I'll think about it," said Stephen. "But do something for me."

"Name it."

"I remember you as someone religious. Get the church open on a Sunday. And give these kids some education."

She smiled. "If the council is up for it, I'll do it."

"The council need all the ideas they can get." He sounded, even to himself, that he was being high-handed, like he was the only one who knew how to do anything. He finished his bitter tea.

39

Council met for a noisy session in the church. No-one objected to Suzanne's proposal to open a school three mornings a week and begin church services on a Sunday led by her. The objections came when Charlie asked for the weapons to be released.

"You just want them for yourself," Gareth's son, Derek, stood up and shouted. Stephen let him get on with it and never moved. Alana placed a hand on his leg.

"I would like them for the soldiers," said Charlie, evenly. "We have been thwarted in collecting wood again. We need the soldiers to protect our wood gathering otherwise it will be a cold winter for sure."

There was some shouting back and forth. Stephen stood up and the shouting subsided. He spoke loudly. His voice rang out in the tall stone building as he leaned on the pew in front. "My recommendation is not to go up there with guns. This Joseph is dangerous. I've seen it in his eyes. Colonel?"

Pullman sat up. She seemed nervous and glanced at Charlie. "I agree it would be dangerous to go." Talbot sat next to her, staring at the floor.

Charlie said, "But we can't go until you release the weapons."

Stephen lifted his hands from the pew and opened his palms in a shrug. There was more shouting and arguing. He knew there was a struggle going on for power. Alana had said it was natural for groups to do this, and that it would pass, but that it would be too dangerous if guns were around. Stephen had agreed and he had decided to hold onto the weapons for now. He certainly did not advocate running up the woods and waving guns about.

Eventually, they left them to it. Gary and Phil were off, patrolling the perimeter, so Stephen took Alana and Karen for a walk. Afternoon chill spread over the village. They took a walk up the street.

Iqbal's shop was open and even doing business. Years before, he had hidden a range of alcohol and tobacco and now felt safe enough to stock his shelves in return for different items. He waved to them from behind his counter as they walked past and they happily waved back, except Karen who continued her solitary appraisal of the world. Stephen had given Iqbal some items they couldn't use like Morgan's boots which were too big for any of them. It felt normal to see a shop open, like it had been yesterday it closed.

After checking the police cell containing the weapons was secure, they came back and crossed over to the burnt-out hall. The soldiers had cleaned it out and made a temporary roof to stable the horses.

They walked inside. It had been organised into stalls for each horse. Sabre was next to Alana's horse, Terror, and Karen's horse which she had renamed Cloud. The soldiers had done well with the building. It was warm and dry. Cloud stuck her head out and Karen petted his nose and fed the horse an apple.

Private Mills was at the far end, filling a metal bucket with water from a tap set in the wall. The tap was small, so he laid the bucket down and wiped his hands on his shoulders. He came up to them, "Cloud's been missing you."

Karen smiled but she kept her attention on the horse. Mills said, "Everything's all ship-shape in here, Miss Karen." He saluted, indulging her role as head of the stables. He grinned and went back to the bucket. The tap coughed but continued to fill the bucket.

From outside, they could hear a roar like a big wave. Stephen rushed outside followed by the girls. The roar continued, loud in the otherwise quiet air. Running over the road to the wash-houses, they rushed up to the wall and looked out to sea, but there was nothing.

"There!" Alana was pointing to the north. Trees rustled and fell over in a wave towards the shore. "It's the Margaretvale River."

At the shoreline where the overflow from the dam met the sea, water started to foam. The river had suddenly increased in volume and it was emptying into the sea. Stephen turned back and went into Gary's old billet. Debris, left over from when they had lived there, was scattered on the floor.

He ran to the sink and twisted the tap. It spluttered some water out but it didn't run. "Dammit." He went back outside. Alana and Karen were looking at the river swelling. A few trees were being swept out and into the current.

Mills came up to them, carrying his metal bucket. "It's half empty. The tap stopped running."

"What's happened?" It was Karen. Alana gaped at her for speaking out loud.

Stephen barely noticed she had spoken. He said, "We have other weapons."

40

IT COULD ONLY have been Joseph's people, thought Stephen. On inspection, the dam's overflow had been opened. Large wheels sat up high on the turf-covered stone wall to control the flow. These wheels had been turned, the dam emptied, and the overflow had been closed again.

No-one in the village understood the water system. They just took it for granted. Now, as the Margaretvale River filled the dam again, they would just have to wait for the pressure to build again. That's if, as Charlie had realised, there's not too much air blocking the system. Added to that was the lack of rain which meant it could be some time before running water was restored.

Stephen had been forced to open the police cell and arm two soldiers to keep watch at the dam. Pullman organised them in shifts to stand guard so the forest folk didn't do it again. She had reported to the Council when it was done.

Stephen went out on patrol with Phil. It was already dark when they left the manse, passed the hall, now already being referred to as The Stables, and up the high street. Phil held his rifle across his front, while Stephen took only his Glock. The barber's and Iqbal's shop were dark and quiet. As was the agreed routine, they checked the doors were secure.

Crossing the road, they passed the old Excise House and Suzanne's place, both with fires on in their front rooms which glowed through their curtains. Phil led them round the village houses. All was quiet with the pleasant smell of wood smoke in the air. They spoke little, enjoying the night air, and not wishing to disturb anyone.

At Rory's old place, Sergeant Talbot was emptying some waste onto his compost heap. He waved and smiled at them. Inside, Colonel Pullman drew the curtains, without seeing them. Satisfied all was fine, they turned back. The

Police Station was undisturbed and the remaining ordnance was still secure in the cell.

"What a night that was," Stephen said to Phil, thinking of when he and Gary had been locked up, and Phil had come to their rescue.

Phil stood in the former reception area. Paul's blood had discoloured the floor. "My Dad told me stories about jailbreaks in the old movies. I just did the same thing."

"Your Dad?"

Phil had said very little about how he had been brought up. He looked at the blood on the floor, as if remembering something else. "We lived in Norham. When Berwick got it..." He trailed off, tightened his lips together, and breathed in through his nose. He blinked at Stephen. "Ready?"

Stephen wanted to say something, but couldn't find the words. He shut the hatch to the cell and walked after Phil as the younger man stepped out onto the street. After locking the blue door, they headed down the lane and trotted down the steps.

Cows shuffled shapes in the dark as they arrived down at the distillery. The tall building narrowed their view of the cloudy sky. All the doors were secure. Phil held his rifle close as Stephen rattled at the doors. "It's a good routine you've put in," said Phil. "Out there, everything's unlocked. Here, security tells us we're safe."

"That's the idea." Stephen leaned on the massive gate which led into the plant. He found himself speaking quietly, despite there being no-one around to disturb. "And it's more than that. We need order. Without it, there's no rules, and bad things happen."

They stepped out to the gap between the buildings. It was completely dark and despite being adjusted to the darkness, they were moving by memory. Phil stopped. "Why did you do it?"

Stephen stopped and turned his back to the sea. Gentle waves brushed through pebbles. "Survival, I think. And then got caught up in it. This was a beautiful place, once."

"Not this, not here," said Phil. "I mean me. Why didn't you kill me that night?" His rifle clicked as he shuffled on his feet.

"I'm glad I didn't," said Stephen.

"Me too." Phil swung his rifle behind him and he embraced Stephen. "You saved my soul."

Overcome, Stephen put his arms round Phil and patted him on the back. Pebbles trickled down the slope of the shore. Water made the sound of a low hollow gulp from the direction of the pier. His blood froze, and Stephen pushed Phil away, grabbed him by the shoulder, and they took cover at the corner of the warehouse.

Whispering in the air, a clunk of wood on stone, and something small clattered on the ground. Phil flashed his rifle torched for an instant at the thing that landed and grabbed it. An arrow, Stephen realised. More whispering as more arrows flew past them, their aim emboldened by the flash of light. Phil ducked behind Stephen, keeping back from the corner.

"We have to go," Stephen hissed. He knew they were under attack, but not from where. He had readied a shot in the Glock. "Back to the stairs."

It was silent again. Stephen puffed a few breaths then ran across the open space, firing into the air. Phil raced after him, firing a few bursts of covering fire into the darkness. Stephen hoped Pullman heard that. They made it to the cover of the distillery.

More arrows slithered through the air. Shadowy figures were gathering at the corner they had just left. Sprinting, they ignored the locked doors. Stephen barged Phil into the side of the wall as arrows clattered off the stone. Phil let out a yell and Stephen felt him drop back. He grabbed at Phil. Phil was bent over, grabbing something at his leg. Stephen felt for it, coming away with blood in his hand and knowing there was an arrow in Phil's leg.

"We have to go," he growled as loud as he dared, sensing shadows all around him. He put himself under Phil's arm and dragged the boy. Somehow, Phil kept his pain in as they moved.

At the end of the distillery, they wheeled round and made it to the stairs. Running footsteps behind them. Arrows thumped into the grass next to them with deadly force. Phil took a sharp intake of breath and went rigid in Stephen's arms.

Stephen laid him down and took the rifle off him. He fired a burst into the darkness, illuminating large figures with short cross-bows in their hands. *We have other weapons*, Stephen thought. Another burst. One of the figures fell. Shouts above Stephen on the stairs. Bursts of fire. Swinging flashlights.

Stephen looked to Phil. He lay there, glassy eyed, an arrow in his throat. Stephen yelled out and fired into the figures again. He was yelling when he felt hands on his collar pulling him back up the stairs. He fired again, the magazine empty, his finger clicking the trigger.

41

"IT'S NOT THE forest folk, then," said Gary as he leaned on the wall in front of the wash-houses. His rifle was slung over his shoulder. Three boats bobbed in the bay. One of them was The Mercury, Malcolm's yacht. They had traded whisky for fish with Malcolm, now he had returned to fetch some more. The other two were smaller sail boats.

Stephen sighed. "And we can say goodbye to the last of the cows too." His eyes felt heavy. He gripped the side of the wall and leaned over. The rocky cliff plunged down to the warehouses where the precious whisky was being plundered. They could hear people moving around down there. The access road to their left was blocked by barrels and men with cross-bows. The stairs were the same; the stairs where Phil died.

Gary sniffed. "How are we going to get these bastards?"

Stephen stayed silent. He couldn't think how to do it and couldn't even look Gary in the eye to tell him. It was Gary who had pulled his collar the night before, dragging him away. O'Neill had dragged Phil's body back, Phil's *body*, while Moore laid down some covering fire.

Their spot at the wash-houses was the best place in the village to see the pier, and even then it was only the edge of the mooring at high tide. Some movement there caught Stephen's eye. He tapped Gary's shoulder and pointed. "On you go, son."

Gary lifted his rifle and eyed the scope. The movement vanished and Gary tutted. "Keep looking," said Stephen. They held the position for a while but nothing re-appeared. Stephen clasped his hand on Gary's shoulder and told him to leave it.

Gary relaxed. "They'll wait until dark."

"So will we, then."

"Hang on." Gary resighted his rifle. Movement on the pier as someone moved then ducked out of sight. Then a rowing boat, pulled by two men moved out into the bay. "That's one of our barrels."

"Take it easy," said Stephen. He could see the dinghy was bigger than the one Malcolm had used, probably big enough for a gang of them to get ashore last night, and now it was heading out to the yachts. Two men were rowing it and on the stern sat perched a barrel of whisky.

Gary breathed out and pulled the trigger. The shot rang out. A few moments later, they could see the men suddenly rowing faster, apparently unharmed. Gary swore.

Stephen clapped him on the back. "Nice try."

Stephen and Gary walked round towards the cattle-grid. As they passed the former hall, now the stables, Stephen's eye caught one of the soldiers in the paddock next to the manse. He was petting Cloud, Karen's horse, and his features were obscured by Terror, who chewed lazily in front of him.

Gary was saying something about the work on the ditch but Stephen kept his eye on the soldier. His boots were muddy and his trousers were in need of a wash, which bothered Stephen because Pullman was normally so strict with them. He stopped Gary by placing a hand on his arm and stepped towards the soldier.

Terror suddenly bucked away, and Cloud followed, revealing the man. He smiled at Stephen. He was about six metres away. Stephen called out, "Gary!"

Immediately, Gary lowered his stance and raised the rifle to his shoulder, targeting the man. Still smiling, the man held his hands out to show he was unarmed. Wearing only a khaki vest-top, above his grubby trousers and boots, he stepped forward. Black lesions dotted his arms and a large purple boil at the neck showed he had the virus.

"Who are you?" Stephen shouted. It had to be one of the soldiers who had deserted all those weeks ago. "Stay right there."

"I am Private Kevin Davis," said the soldier. He slowed but did not stop. Keeping his hands outstretched, he kept moving towards them.

Gary shifted his position. "What will I do?"

"Don't shoot him," said Stephen, holding out a hand in warning. "But keep him covered."

Davis halted about two metres from them. He dropped his smile and closed his eyes and leant his head back. Breathing deeply through his nose, he seemed content while the purple boil stretched and pulsed. Stephen pulled Gary by the shoulder to move him around, away from the cattle grid. From a window in the manse, Alana dragged Karen away from the window.

Davis blew air out gently between pursed lips. He opened his eyes and turned to face Stephen. "We have other weapons."

Stephen shivered. *We have other weapons.* Joseph had told him that in the woods. He had meant the virus, Stephen realised, and this was Joseph sending it into the Village.

"Don't worry," said Davis. His smile had returned, chilling despite its intended warmth. "I'm not here to hurt you."

"Then why are you here?" Stephen was afraid of the answer.

Davis shrugged. "Just stay out the forest. It's ours." He started to back off towards the cattle-grid. He let his hands drop to his side.

"Stay on him." Stephen tapped Gary on the shoulder and they advanced.

Davis stopped. He looked around, thinking. "I think I'll go for a swim." He turned and walked slowly to the edge of the village.

Stephen tried to think what he meant. This was a warning from Joseph, to stay away, but he had sent someone with the virus only for him to walk away. Then he got it. "Do not let him in the reservoir!"

They followed Davis out the village. Silently, he left as quietly as he had arrived. They did not dare let him near the water supply. They killed him and burned his body when it was far enough away from the village.

42

THEY MET IN the church. Pullman and Talbot left their weapons in the entranceway and came in. Stephen and Gary sat facing Charlie and Frank. Alana sat quietly behind Stephen holding both Karen's hands. The soldiers sat down between the two pairs, making a square cornered U-shape.

Charlie smiled at the soldiers and thanked them for coming. He turned back to Stephen and said, "Again. I think we should ask the others."

Stephen said, "This is a war council."

Charlie snorted. "War council?"

"What else do you call it when you're invaded and your resources are being stolen?"

"Piracy?" Charlie offered. Frank shuffled in his seat.

"Charlie, you're arguing over wording? And not to mention what just happened with Private Davis." Stephen shook his head. He felt like he didn't have the energy for this, despite just shouting at Charlie. He just wanted to go somewhere and cry about Ellen and Jack. And Phil, who lay in the cold vestry.

"Stephen," said Frank, and gestured around the building. "The church."

Stephen looked at him with weary eyes, knowing his expression was dark. Frank stared back at him, the way Stephen's own father had when he was thinking "I've already bloody told you."

Stephen let it go. "Charlie, the village will do what you recommend. These soldiers will do what we ask of them."

Pullman and Talbot didn't respond directly but they glanced at each other. Stephen wondered where their loyalties would lie if it came to choosing sides. Charlie said, "Except perhaps hurl themselves at a hail of arrows."

"Agreed," said Stephen and looked at the floor. He felt Phil gasp and go stiff in his arms all over again. "But I want that bastard Malcolm's boat holed, burned and sunk."

Everyone looked at each other, nervously. Frank spoke first. "It might be better if we could capture one of the boats for our own needs."

"Are you kidding?" Stephen knew he was right but he couldn't help himself being angry. Frank swallowed and sat back.

Pullman tried to sound reasonable. "Before we decide which of those options we prefer. We need a plan for how to get down there."

Stephen said, "Any ideas?"

"I've got it," said Gary, without waiting for Pullman to respond. "The road and steps are out of order. But we go down the cliff in front of the wash-houses."

Talbot said, "It could be done. You done it before?"

Gary shrugged. He hadn't but he tried to make it look like he had.

Pullman interjected, "What about the water?" They all looked at her. She went on, "We go out the village, down the river, and round the point onto the shore."

Stephen looked at Charlie, who turned the sides of his mouth down in agreement. Stephen shook his head. "It's too far. The water's too cold."

"After dark it will be low tide again," said Alana. Stephen turned round and glared at her. She ignored him. "And something else to consider when you're aiming at those boats. If you steal them, or hole them, where do your pirates go then?"

"Who cares?" said Stephen.

She sighed and looked at him. "They will stand and fight if you force them to. Make them flee, or there will be more casualties."

Charlie and Frank looked uncomfortable at his and Alana's exchange. Stephen turned his back to her. "Right. We need a plan. Either we leave them to take what they want, and we've got another Morgan on our hands, or we do something about it."

Talbot eyed Stephen. "And what about Joseph?"

"We'll take care of him afterwards," said Stephen, eyeing Talbot back.

Alana spoke again. "You can't beat him, you know." Stephen said nothing. He looked at the roof, his jaw slightly forward. Alana went on, "He's a fanatic. His people are fanatics. Davis walked down here to die. Just like that."

Talbot looked to Pullman and the two of them watched the floor.

"What do you suggest?" Charlie asked.

Alana sat forward. "Keep out of his forest. It's his."

Charlie leaned forward. "We need wood."

"It's his," Alana said again, ice in her tone. "Didn't you hear him?"

43

L IGHT WAS FADING. Two more yachts had moored up in the bay. Their decision had been made for the villagers. The boats were not going to just fill up and leave. This wasn't going to be like before. Boats and men would keep coming until the warehouses were empty and when they had more men, they might think about what else the village had to offer them.

Stephen sat in the kitchen, checking his weapons. He had cleaned the Glock and had reassembled it, taking Alana's advice not to oil it too much. His knife was clean and sat on the table. Karen sat watching him, drinking in every detail of what he was doing. Alana leaned against the worktop sipping nettle tea.

"There is another option, you know," she said.

He tried ignoring her after showing him up like that at the meeting. Despite knowing she was right, she had undermined him in front of the others. Eventually, when he realised she was waiting for him to respond, he asked, "Which is?"

She spoke to him gently. "Forget it. Leave. We'll all go together."

Something caught in his throat and he swallowed. It was inconceivable that he should leave but he found it hard to explain, even to himself, what motivated him. He had arrived here only three months ago, for the first time in years, and now it was about to taken away from him. But it wasn't his village to be taken from him, he realised. It was Ellen's.

She gestured with her mug. "I'm going to saddle up Cloud and Terror. If things get bad, we're going."

Stephen almost threw the gun on the table. He felt so defeated. He lowered his head, stretching his fingers as his palms rested on the table. Alana sat down beside him and placed a hand on his. "It's my son," he said, suddenly understanding why he was doing this.

"Phil?" Alana tried to soothe him with her voice.

"No," said Stephen, lifting his head and meeting her eyes. "It's my son, Jack."

He had told Alana nothing of his life before meeting her, and all he knew of her was her job as a Forensic Psychologist. It was as if, clinging to each other in the dark, their past lives would have encroached on the new. He said, "I was away with work."

Alana shifted in her chair and she swallowed. She looked at Karen, considering sending her out the room, but she kept quiet. Wide-eyed, Karen watched. Stephen told them everything.

He had been a lorry driver in 2015 on a run to Manchester. Living with Ellen and Jack in Dumfries, he took for granted that they would be there when he got back, even when things were turning bad. The virus hadn't quite gotten a grip, but already the Scottish Government had taken over the businesses. Along with three other trucks, he was hauling water south to the boundary of the infected zone.

The wall at Carlisle, which ran across the M74, was garrisoned by the army. They checked his paperwork and waved the convoy through. From there, they were escorted along the M6 by more soldiers. It gave Stephen the feeling that his family were safe back in Scotland.

Everything was uneventful until they got to Preston. A roadblock, of cars and concrete blocks, was set up where the motorway joined the M61. Even without petrol rationing, and there being little traffic, travel restrictions meant the roads had been clear until that point. A roadblock meant bad news.

It turned out the infected zone had become worse and the roadblock had been set up by a rogue police unit who wanted the water for themselves. A fire fight broke out between the police and soldiers. Stephen had made it out of his cab, somehow unhurt, and fled on foot. One of the soldiers had been shot, and while he lay on the ground dying, Stephen grabbed at a pistol and ran.

It took him a long time to get back. He found some kindness, people who shared some food, but he also found cruelty as things broke down. Having taught himself how to use the pistol he killed his first man outside Staveley Train Station over nothing. It was raining. The man had been standing in a doorway and had followed Stephen down the street. It was dark with no-one else around. He had shoved Stephen in the back and he had tried to ignore him but he kept on pushing for no reason. Stephen had stumbled into the building on the corner. He looked up at the sign attached to the wall: fading and water damaged, it was the timetable for trains which no longer ran.

Stephen felt for the gun in his pocket. He just rammed it into the man's chest, released the safety and pulled the trigger. The recoil grazed his hand between thumb and forefinger. The man's face was surprised and he just fell back.

Stephen ran. He must have dropped the pistol because he never saw it again. He kept going. When he finally reached the wall at Carlisle, there were no troops; no-one at all. Eventually, he made it back to Dumfries, back to his house, and his life. But when he got there, he froze. He felt dizzy and his legs were heavy. Ellen and Jack were gone.

It looked like Ellen had tried to pack. Their holiday suitcase had some things in it but she hadn't finished the job. The case just lay there; open, with a few clothes neatly rolled in the base. The house was empty; the whole street was empty, like everyone had cleared out. Next door, their neighbour had stabbed his wife and children with a kitchen knife and hung himself in the garden. As the neighbour swung there in the breeze, flies buzzed about the inside of the house. He had lived there for two years and Stephen didn't even know their names.

There was no-one to tell him what had happened. Dead bodies in the street and houses signified the virus had hit but no sign of Ellen and Jack. Over time, he heard rumours that the army had evacuated the whole of Galloway. But Stephen had kept searching, going to places where he thought they might be until he had arrived here, at the village, where Ellen had grown up.

"I thought she might have come home, you see?" he said in the kitchen of the manse. "I can't imagine them dead, because then what's the point? But I can't imagine them alive, because then that's worse."

Alana blew air out between tight lips, keeping it together. She looked at Karen gravely; imagining, or remembering, who knows what, thought Stephen. He went on, "I'm sorry I never told you any of this, but I thought if I reveal my old life, it's like I'm admitting it's over. I have to fight to keep going so I'll find Jack again."

Alana got up and moved over to the window. She leaned on the sink and her shoulders began to tremble. Karen watched her quietly, as if used to it.

"And I know it is over," said Stephen. He listened to himself and saw his whole life for the past five years. Finding two decayed bodies near Morpeth had seemed like the lowest point. Two police officers lying forgotten in a field, overcome by the virus, not even buried. He had sat with them for a while, thinking of their lives, wondering if they had been good people. He made his mind up they must have been exceptional officers and, having fallen in their duty, that their tragic deaths somehow symbolised what everyone had lost. He had hoped for something new then, a better future. He had lifted their police issue Glocks, one of which lay on the table in front of him. He told Alana this as she stayed bent over the sink, tears falling onto the porcelain.

Then he said, "Be prepared. Saddle the horses. I have to

do this one last thing. And when I get back... Alana."

He reached out to her and she came back to sit beside him. She curled up on the chair. He took her hand and reached out for Karen with the other. Reluctantly, she took it.

He said, "When I get back, Alana, I want to you to be my wife. And Karen, I want you to be our daughter."

Karen withdrew her hand. Stephen knew why, because it was one of the few things Alana had told him, in an effort to make him understand her silence. "And Karen, when your Mummy and Daddy come to get you, you will go with them. Until then, you'll live with us."

Stephen suddenly had it all planned in his head. Suzanne would bless them in the church and they could live in the village together. "Gary is already my son," he said. "And you will be with us, safe."

Karen reached out for Stephen's hand.

44

NIGHT ARRIVED. GARY lowered a rope down the cliff. Dave braced it against the wall. Stephen positioned the rifle on his back as he leaned over, holding the rope. After tapping Stephen on the shoulder, Frank placed a pair of night vision goggles over his head. Previously the property of Colonel Morgan, Frank used them to scan the narrow gap between the West Warehouse and cliff. None of them spoke.

Underneath the cliff, a narrow access path behind the warehouses was covered in pebbles dredged from the beach. It would mean they should hear someone moving about down there, but Frank was to keep watch all the same. Stephen began to lower himself down. With no experience of repelling down a rope, he had to walk down and just hold on.

Crumbly and jagged, the cliff spilled some loose flaked stones to the bottom. Now between the rock face and the three storey warehouse, Stephen paused. There was no sound from below and Frank had not cleared his throat, their agreed signal. He was half way down, sweating badly into his eyes and his hands hurt, but Stephen kept on.

He stepped gently onto the pebbles, feeling them settle quietly under his boots, and shook the rope to signal Gary to follow. Stephen crouched down and shrugged off the rifle. He held it up to his shoulder and looked in both directions. All was quiet and dark, sheltered between the cliff and building.

The rope twisted and snaked on the ground as Gary made his way down. In the middle storey of the warehouse, a light went on and pale illumination leaked out between the bars and onto the cliff face. The rope stopped moving.

Stephen lifted himself up and pointed his rifle at the window. Covered in a thick metal grill, the window could not be opened or seen through from inside, but Stephen took the precaution anyway. There were voices inside and some light laughter before the light went out. Stephen breathed out. The rope snaked around again.

Finally, Gary made it to the ground. He tugged twice on the rope and it slithered up the cliff away from them. Gary readied his rifle. Stephen tapped him on the shoulder and they crept along to the corner of the building. Stephen crouched down and stuck one eye round the corner. There was no movement.

Gary had followed him to this spot, having moved backwards to cover their position. Stephen tapped him again and Gary moved passed the corner into a hollow under the cliff, opposite the warehouse corner.

Gary turned and backed in. Stephen did the same and the two of them hunkered down, secure in the darkness. They waited.

Morning was on its way. Gary was chittering beside Stephen. Stephen looked at his watch. It was nearly time. During the night, they had been undisturbed in their damp corner. They had seen a few men stagger back and forth along the road, nice and drunk, while they themselves were unseen in the dark behind the warehouse.

They readied themselves by standing and shaking out their feet. Gary shook his head and let his cheek flap about. Stephen yawned and checked his equipment. Former Colonel Morgan had bequeathed him two grenades, now attached to his belt, and he wondered if they would work. Cracks sounded out, breaking the silence. From their cave, they could not be sure of the direction, but they had been expecting it from the south; the stairs. Moore and Gibson, they both knew, were taking pot-shots at the barricade at the bottom of the stairs.

The two soldiers had spent the night crawling by inches to a position where they could do the most damage. O'Neill and Mills were in support at their rear, to protect the men, but ready to storm the barricade if necessary or able. That four-man group was the beginnings of a diversion and it was working. From their position, Gary and Stephen saw two men trot past the opening at the road, running south.

Without speaking, Stephen led the way. They stepped lightly on the gravel with their weapons at their shoulders. At the end of the warehouse, they kept low while Stephen peered over to the barricade at the bottom of the access road. Piled high with barrels, two men remained on guard, but looked away from the road, passed Stephen, towards the action at the stairs. They were too far to see anything, and it was still dark, but Stephen could make out the men were anxiously trying to make out what was happening.

Perfect, thought Stephen. He glanced at Gary, determination on his face. They waited. In the dark, they heard a dull groan and something slumped onto the ground. Something else slid off a barrel and lay beside it. It was both men from the barrel barricade, having been injured or killed, by two figures now running to the East Warehouse. Facing the sea, the long building provided cover for the two and they hunkered down at the wall. Stephen recognised their forms. It was Pullman and Talbot, who had used the time to take advantage of the low tide and make their way across the shoreline. Part of the backup plan was for Gary and Stephen to provide support for them if they failed or were compromised in any way.

As agreed, Pullman and Talbot lined up cover down the road south. Stephen and Gary were first out. In between the tall buildings, they ran down the quiet street before ducking into the first doorway. They took up a firing position while Pullman and Talbot ran past them and ducked into a doorway on the left. Up ahead, there were men running towards the pier away from the gunfire. The shots were clearer here and sound bounced between the buildings. Stephen and Gary made off to the next door and again covered while Pullman and Talbot took up their final spot.

Stephen quickly looked around. They were alone. There was still some confusion up ahead and he didn't want to run into any gunfire. If the four man team had managed to progress, they were to funnel the men towards the pier and their escape; Alana's plan allowing them to escape and minimise the fighting. The risk for them now was in running into a bullet. He glanced over at Pullman and Talbot, patiently covering the area in front of the large gate.

Up ahead, one man ran, pulling his trousers up. In the gloom, Stephen thought it was Malcolm, the sailor they had previously traded whisky for fish. Stephen went after him, with Gary at his heel. They reached the corner of the building facing the sea. Keeping low, Stephen stuck his head round. Behind them, they heard Pullman and Talbot take up a new position.

All the men, seven in all, had gathered on the moorings at the pier-end and were waiting for one of the yachts which was heading in. Two men on a smaller boat furiously rowed out to their vessel.

The sky was beginning to lighten in the east and Stephen could make out that the approaching yacht was The Mercury, Malcolm's craft, heading towards the pier. A second yacht had lifted its anchor and was following into the moorings. Malcolm himself shuffled his feet as he waited, nervously looking behind him, almost dancing. Stephen made way for Gary, a much better shot. He pointed out Malcolm and Gary nodded a quick agreement as he sighted the rifle.

Gary breathed out and squeezed the trigger. Malcolm went down and the others on the pier panicked. Three men dived into the water and started swimming. The Mercury kept coming and bumped into the mooring. Malcolm's companion threw out a line for one man to catch. It was Malcolm, back on his feet, but hopping on one leg, the other trailing uselessly beside him.

Two men took up defensive positions, low down in the stone part of the pier, and fired off arrows from small cross-bows. Wood clattered on the cement ground as the arrows landed harmlessly out of range. Stephen rounded the corner keeping low, and fired off a shot which landed who knows where, but had the effect of making the two men with cross-bows retreat. They joined the final man who helped Malcolm steady the boat against the mooring.

Seeing the men clamber onto the boat, Stephen moved quickly. Keeping his knees bent, he moved fast towards the pier. Gary was beside him. As they stepped onto the pier, an arrow slipped by him, sounding lethal and in range, but miraculously missed. Stephen fired at the yacht, hoping to hole it.

The Mercury began to slip away from the side. Malcolm was trying to lift his damaged leg into his boat but the other men were barging past him. He slipped and fell into the water as the gap between boat and mooring widened. Gary fired and the men on the boat ducked down and hid, some making it below. Out in the water, the swimmers had made it to the second yacht and were being hauled aboard. Malcolm's friend was reaching down trying to lift him out the water but Malcolm was floundering, panicking and shouting.

The sky had begun to turn grey as the sun threatened to lift above the horizon. Stephen came forward again and fired. Malcolm let go of the side of the boat but continued to thrash in the water. Gary was firing again as Stephen reached for his belt and found one of the grenades. He pulled the pin, and threw it over arm, like Talbot had shown him. He heard a knocking sound he hoped was the grenade bouncing on the deck and Gary was pulling at his shoulder.

They ran up the pier and the grenade went off. It was not as huge an explosion as Stephen had expected but he felt the force of it in his back thump him forward. He stumbled but Gary had him by the arm and they stayed upright. Stopping running, Stephen turned back to the boat. The blast had blown open the far side of the hull and the whole craft lurched around as water flooded in.

A couple of men had made it off the boat and were swimming to the second yacht which had now made its turn and was sailing away from them. The other boats, which had moored in the bay, had begun to turn and were fleeing.

Followed by Gary, Stephen ran to the mooring's end. Spluttering, and slapping around in the water, Malcolm was making his way to the edge. He stopped when he saw Stephen looming over him. He was distraught and afraid, which pleased Stephen. Out in the bay, The Mercury was sinking. Its mast was undamaged and poked up to the brightening sky. There was no sign of anyone else. The swimmers were still chasing the second yacht.

Above his hip, Stephen held the rifle. He pointed it towards Malcolm, who froze and waited in the water, his hair soaked and matted. Gary watched him, impassively.

"No!" The shout was from behind Stephen. It was Pullman. Backed by Talbot and the other four soldiers, she held her hand out in a halting gesture. Stephen locked eyes with her, his rifle still pointing at Malcolm, and pulled the trigger.

45

SABRE, MORGAN'S FORMER horse, and now
belonging to Stephen, pulled Frank's trailer. She didn't like
it, but she did it. Frank led her by the reins as they made
their way up the forest path. Stephen walked in front, with
no rifle, just his Glock and the hunting knife tucked in their
holster and sheath. Dave walked behind, ready to lean on
the trailer if it got stuck, but the dry weather meant the
going was good.

On the trailer was a barrel of whisky. White oak in
construction, it contained just under two-hundred litres of
single malt Glen Craobhmore. Frank coaxed Sabre up the
hill under the strain. He had complained about the journey,
saying the horse would not be up to it, and Stephen had
sensed the older man's own fear, but had managed to talk
him round. Frank's expertise with the barrels was needed.

As they headed by the reservoir, they ignored checking
whether it was filling up or not and kept on. Eventually,
they neared the forest edge and found the barrier
unmanned. It took the three of them to move it back,
despite it being a little dilapidated. After moving it, Stephen
looked at the branches which made up the gate. The last
time he had been here, the barrier was new, but despite it
only being a short time later it was starting to look decayed.
He wondered what this was telling him, but Frank had
gotten Sabre moving again, and he didn't find any time to
consider it further.

As they moved further into the forest, light dappled
between the branches onto the path and they began to
smell wood smoke from the camp's fires. Nearing, the
settlement, Stephen noticed another smell. A rotten stench
threaded in between the aromas of the camp. Frank and
Dave eyed each other nervously. Stephen strode on.

Joseph's tent, the yurt, sat grey and quiet in the middle
of the camp. Faces hid behind trees or ducked inside their

own tents and make-shift shelters leaning against trees. Stephen looked around, unsettled by the atmosphere. Before, the people had been quiet, but their silent defiance had sparked the air. This time, they seemed afraid and restrained. A child of about five chased a dog through the trees, her joy in contrast to everything else.

Trees had been felled to create more space. Jagged stumps poked about the camp. Finally, they faced Joseph's tent. The tartan rugs hung across the door in front of a small fire which burned brightly in the dark corner of the forest. Filthy, and showing signs of wear, one rug was gripped at the edge and Joseph emerged.

He smiled on recognising Stephen. "You've brought different friends." Frank and Dave huddled next to Sabre. He looked to his left as if looking for one of his followers to be pushing Talbot into the camp again. Stephen said nothing. Joseph turned to his right, and made the same show of searching the trees.

Stephen baulked but he did not move. On Joseph's neck was a swollen, purple, boil. Dave went to back off, but Frank got a hold of him. He made the younger man begin to release the horse from the trailer. Joseph touched the boil, self-consciously, and turned back to Stephen, smiling again.

Stephen looked around. A family huddled inside in a small lean-to, boils on their necks; the virus. Joseph spoke again. "To what do I owe the pleasure?"

Stephen said, "We've brought a peace offering." He gestured as Dave moved Sabre away from the trailer and walked her back down the hill.

Joseph saw the barrel. "We have no need of your whisky. We have the forest."

Stephen paused. He moved towards Joseph, who backed up and looked around for someone to help him. Having no wish to get too close to Joseph, Stephen kept the fire between them. "Shame about Private Davis."

Joseph eyes crinkled into an unrepentant smile and Stephen saw madness there. A large man lumbered out from behind the tent and stood behind Joseph. He seemed untouched by the virus himself and untroubled by being near it. Stephen understood in that moment that they would never be free of them, that their devotion to Joseph was like a sickness worse than the virus. He glanced at Frank, fussing around the barrel, and noticed the big man lick his lips at the thought of the spirit inside.

Dave led the horse down the hill with no-one bothering him. Stephen turned back to Joseph. "This whisky is yours. I'm going to give it to you."

Itching to reach for his gun and shoot Joseph, Stephen looked at the bigger man and wondered what would happen next. Frank rammed the barrel's cork bung with his corkscrew tool and twisted it a few times. The bigger man was licking his lips again and stepped away from his leader. Stephen smiled at Stephen. With a practiced calm, Frank pulled the bung out; its sack cloth wrap fell to the ground. Whisky began to glug out the opening. Joseph frowned. Stephen picked a burning log from the fire and walked to the barrel.

The big man saw what he was doing, but Stephen had drawn his pistol and aimed it at the man's chest, backing up towards the trailer, halting the bigger man. Frank had jumped back as the spirit poured onto the ground. It formed a large puddle which trickled outwards down the path. Whisky fumes in the air, pungent and warm, mixed pleasingly with the wood smoke.

Stephen dropped the log down into the spirit. The vapour caught light and burned pale blue. He kept the pistol on the big man and moved further back. There was panic in Joseph's eyes and he seemed paralysed to act. Frustrated at the lack of orders, the big man retreated behind Joseph's tent and came back with a bucket, heavy with water.

Stephen shot the man in the chest and he fell back. The bucket bounced and the water splashed onto the tent. The whisky was starting to burn further. The barrel was emptying though its position on the trailer meant probably only a third of it would leak out of the barrel. People came out of their tents but, seeing what had happened to their comrade, declined to intervene, and started to gather their things to move.

Flames were beginning to catch in the dry settlement. Stephen backed off, still aiming at people he saw. Frank had hobbled quickly down the path after Dave and Sabre. Joseph watched them silently, a mad smile in his eyes. Stephen saw him once more through the flames and the thickening smoke.

46

The forest burned brightly for two days until finally heavy rain, the first for months, came in from the west before the fire could catch further down the hill. It had lit up the night sky. A few refugees made it to the village and were quarantined in the church until they could show they were not infected. There was no sign of Joseph.

Lying in bed with Alana next to him, Stephen was awakened by a loud knock on the door. Startled, he bolted up. Alana was ahead of him and gathered Karen to her in the bathroom. Stephen ran to the front room where Gary was looking out the window. Still in his shorts, Gary gestured casually with his thumb.

Stephen looked out. Charlie was standing in the garden looking up. Behind him were Pullman and Talbot, holding their rifles across their fronts. Moore and Gibson had taken up positions to the left and right, their rifles ready at their cheeks, pointing up at them. A look out the back window showed O'Neill and Mills in a similar position.

Charlie shouted up, "It's time, Stephen." His voice was muffled by the window, but they heard the words and understood their meaning. It was the day after Phil's funeral; at least they had waited for that, thought Stephen.

Stephen opened the door and they all stepped out. O'Neill and Mills had rounded the house, from the back, and trained their weapons on the group. Talbot and Moore had closed in. Behind them, Pullman and Talbot supervised their men. Charlie stood behind them. "It's time for you to go, Stephen."

They had gathered together their belongings, including all their tins and carried them across their bags on army packs. They waited by the door, calm and restrained. Stephen breathed in through his nose, and walked forward, but not quickly, so as not to startle the soldiers.

He went towards Charlie. Moore and Gibson tracked back, all the while their weapons on him, while the rest were covered by O'Neill and Mills. Charlie swallowed. Pullman and Talbot stayed in position, and kept their attention on Stephen, but did not make their weapons ready. This told Stephen they genuinely wanted him to leave and not start a fight; a lesson learned from Alana perhaps.

Stephen reached Pullman. "Colonel?"

Pullman looked him in the eye and he saw the soldier there, professional and sure. For the first time, she wore the two silver pistols at her waist. "You told me the council were the Government."

Stephen glanced at Talbot before giving his attention to Charlie, who said, "You'll leave your guns and horses."

Stephen turned the sides of his mouth down and shook his head. He waited. Her attention still on Stephen, Pullman said, "Sergeant Talbot."

Talbot nodded once. "Yes, ma'am. Gibson! Moore! The stables!"

The two soldiers lowered their weapons and double-timed it over to the former village hall. Stephen kept staring at Charlie. He was raging inside and wanted to smack him in the teeth but found comfort in the uneasy look on Charlie's face as the soldiers returned with four horses; one on each hand and already saddled. This had all been planned. Stephen imagined Charlie saying he wanted them to leave with nothing, while Pullman argued they might fight otherwise, and arranging the backup plan.

Alana and Karen ran forward where Alana helped Karen onto Cloud before she in turn mounted Terror. Gary mounted his horse and held the reins of Sabre. Gibson and Moore melted back but readied their rifles. Alana quickly led Karen away towards the cattle grid which they navigated around.

"Good luck, Charlie," said Stephen. He took the reins from Gary and pulled himself up onto the saddle. He looked at Colonel Pullman. She patted Sabre's neck and, with only a nod of her head, she wished Stephen luck.

Without looking back, Stephen trotted Sabre round the cattle grid and around the gate. The ditches had never been finished and it was simple to reach the road. Gareth and Derek manned the gate, avoiding Stephen's eyes as he passed.

As they headed up the road, away from the village, Stephen saw Suzanne in her back garden, waving. He raised an arm in reply and clicked his horse to catch up with Alana and Karen. Gary trotted behind.